California
Crazy

Books by Beverly Lewis

GIRLS ONLY (GO!)
Youth Fiction

Dreams on Ice	Follow the Dream
Only the Best	Better Than Best
A Perfect Match	Photo Perfect
Reach for the Stars	Star Status

SUMMERHILL SECRETS
Youth Fiction

Whispers Down the Lane	House of Secrets
Secret in the Willows	Echoes in the Wind
Catch a Falling Star	Hide Behind the Moon
Night of the Fireflies	Windows on the Hill
A Cry in the Dark	Shadows Beyond the Gate

HOLLY'S HEART
Youth Fiction

Best Friend, Worst Enemy	California Crazy
Secret Summer Dreams	Second-Best Friend
Sealed With a Kiss	Good-Bye, Dressel Hills
The Trouble With Weddings	Straight-A Teacher

www.BeverlyLewis.com

California
Crazy

Beverly Lewis

BETHANYHOUSE
Minneapolis, Minnesota

Published by Bethany House Publishers
A Ministry of Bethany Fellowship International
11400 Hampshire Avenue South
Bloomington, Minnesota 55438
www.bethanyhouse.com

Printed in the United States of America by
Bethany Press International, Bloomington, Minnesota 55438

Library of Congress Cataloging-in-Publication Data

Lewis, Beverly, 1949–
    California crazy / by Beverly Lewis.
        p.   cm. — (Holly's heart ; 5)
Rewritten version of: California Christmas. Grand Rapids, Mich. :
Zondervan, c1994.
Summary: When she goes to visit her father in California for Christmas,
Holly has to deal with her feelings about the boyfriend she leaves
behind in Colorado, her snoopy younger sister, and her new stepmother.
    ISBN 0-7642-2504-9
    [1. Stepfamilies—Fiction.   2. Christian life—Fiction.
3. Christmas—Fiction.]   I. Title.
    PZ7.L58464   Can   2002
    [Fic]—dc21

                                                        2002002800

Author's Note

Big hugs to my teen consultants, who always have wonderful ideas.

Thanks to my SCBWI writers' group, and to my husband, Dave, whose loving support and super sandwiches make this series possible.

Special thanks to B. J. Reinhard for her information on Labradors.

To

Lori Walburg VandenBosch,

my very first editor

and dear friend.

1

Happily ever after? Right! I thought as I locked the upstairs bathroom door. Two weeks ago, Mom had married Uncle Jack, and our perfectly peaceful surroundings changed overnight. Now my boy cousins—Stan, Phil, and Mark— were brousins, as in cousins-turned-stepbrothers. What a shock adding three boys to an all-girl household! To top it off, their seven-year-old sister, Stephie, was a spoiled brat and the biggest little snoop around.

I stared at the bathroom mirror, furiously brushing my hair. Our house on Downhill Court—the house Daddy had built—was now crawling with people. Stan, fifteen, had claimed the queen-sized sofa bed in the family room. Phil, ten, and Mark, eight, had invaded Carrie's bedroom, forcing me to share my room with two super snoopers: Carrie, nine, and Stephie, also known as the "baby" of our newly blended family.

Mom and Uncle Jack were the only ones who didn't seem to mind the crowded conditions. In the time it took for them to say "I do," my life had been altered forever!

"Holly!" Carrie pounded on the bathroom door. "Hurry up!"

"Hey, I just got in here," I yelled through the door.

"Did not," she called back. "You've been hogging the bathroom all morning."

Hmm, I thought. *Carrie's acting more like Stephie every day. Bratty!*

I sighed and ignored the banging. Not only was the house overrun with zillions of people, my bedroom was now cluttered with personal belongings times three! And to top it off, my window seat was practically defunct—at least for quiet times and journal writing. Its latest function was to serve as Stephie's bed. Pillows, stuffed animals, and blankets were piled up in both corners of my beloved spot. Carrie's bed was a fold-up cot, stashed in a corner of the room during the daytime.

Staring back at the mirror, I longed for the quiet days, before Jack Patterson and company moved to Dressel Hills, Colorado, our fabulous ski village in the heart of the Rockies.

"Holly!" Carrie shouted. "Mom wants you downstairs right now!"

"Nice try," I hollered back. "Mom's out Christmas shopping with Uncle Jack." They were also buying groceries. Saturdays were grocery-buying days. Now that Mom was remarried, there was a man instead of me to lug the groceries to the car—one of the real advantages of having a stepdad.

"I just saw Mommy," Carrie insisted.

"Yeah," I muttered, "in your dreams."

"Holly!" Stephie joined the campaign. "If you don't come out now, I'll wet my pants!"

"*That's* an interesting approach," I said, laughing but feeling slightly guilty. "Why don't you use the bathroom downstairs?"

Stephie turned up the whine. "Stan's combing his hair in there."

"Yeah," Carrie blurted. "And he said if we didn't disappear, he'd turn us into cat food."

"Sisters . . . brothers," I whispered. "What a perfect nightmare."

"Go back downstairs and bug Stan some more," I suggested, posing in the mirror as I pulled my long blond hair away from my face. "Maybe he's finished primping by now."

"But what about the cat food?" Stephie asked.

I sighed, exasperated. "Look, Christmas is

coming soon, and Santa doesn't bring toys to kids who bug their big sisters."

That got them. Quickly the girls scampered down the stairs.

"Good riddance," I whispered, reaching for my makeup bag. Lightly applying brown mascara, I remembered the fabulous lavender bedroom—exclusively mine—before the Patterson takeover. My private dresser drawer, the bottom one where I kept my writing, had to go. Mom insisted it be cleaned out to make room for Carrie's clothes. So . . . good-bye to secret storage of journals, short stories, and pen pal letters. Now my writing notebooks were boxed up and stored under my canopy bed, the safest place I could find. For now.

The day after Mom's wedding, I had purchased a diary that locked. It was the only possible way to maintain my secrecy. I'd hidden the key in this bathroom, safely tucked away under a flower arrangement on top of the white wicker cabinet above the toilet. Who would think of looking up there for a diary key?

I glanced at the cabinet on the wall. *The super snoopers will never find it,* I thought, feeling smug. But, of course, it wouldn't hurt to double-check. Standing on tiptoes in my new brown suede boots, I positioned my feet on the toilet lid. It wiggled under my feet, so I lifted the lid and seat for a sturdier base. Couldn't afford to crack the seat and get stuck paying for it now that my savings were totally wiped out. But, glancing down at the cool boots, I didn't mind the depleted funds. They were worth every penny I'd spent.

Bam! Something outside bashed against the bathroom door. I flinched. "Is that you, Carrie?"

"If you don't want to be responsible for this door getting knocked down, you'd better open it now!" my sister shouted.

"Just hold on," I said, steadying myself. "Give me two seconds."

"Okay," she said, "I'm counting. One one-thousand, two one-thousand. Time's up!"

I thought the door would cave in from the pounding, and then, miraculously, the doorbell rang. Carrie scrambled downstairs. Good, privacy at last!

I reached for the top of the wicker cabinet and grabbed Mom's fancy new Christmas arrangement. One little peek under the arrangement would assure me of the diary key's safety. I stood on tiptoes, stretching, reaching . . .

And then it happened—my right foot slipped. I grabbed for the wall, anything, to stop my fall, but I was well on my way into the toilet. Well, not all of me, just my foot. I squealed as the cold water sloshed up over my socks and halfway up my leg. The icy cold water was bad enough, but . . . Yikes, my expensive boot!

I stared at the brown suede boot, now soaked with toilet water. So much for the totally cool look. Then I tried to pull my foot out.

It was stuck.

"Help!" I screamed, ready to yell that I was caught in the toilet, but that sounded really dumb. Instead, I stared, horrified, at the curvy narrow part of the toilet where the sole of the boot was trapped. I shuddered, wishing I'd worn my bedroom slippers instead. Wiggling my toes, I tried to free my foot from the toilet's grasp, but it was no use.

Mom and Uncle Jack were gone from the house. Stan was primping in the bathroom off the family room, two levels below. Phil and Mark were playing at a friend's house—which meant Carrie and Stephie were my only hope.

I took a deep breath and called for them. "Carrie! Stephie! The bathroom's free!" There, that should get an immediate response.

Leaning my head toward the door, I listened. I balanced myself with my left foot and held on to the sink with my left hand. "Carrie!" I called again.

Nothing. The house was perfectly still. Funny, when you *wanted* someone around, this place was as dead as dried-up pine needles.

"Anybody home?" I shouted at the top of my lungs.

My shouting was met with silence. What could I do? How long before someone would need to use this bathroom? For the first time in my life, I wished we were a one-bathroom house.

Staring down at my cold, soggy foot, I resisted the momentary urge to reach into the water and unzip my boot. *Nah,* I thought. I wiggled my foot again. Even with my boot unzipped, I was sure I couldn't get my foot out of the toilet.

Br-r-ring—the phone! My heart sank as I checked my watch. One thirty-three. It was probably Jared Wilkins, the coolest guy in Dressel Hills Junior High.

The church youth group Christmas party was only two weeks away. Was Jared calling to ask me? I was dying to know. Of course, it's a little tricky to answer the hall phone, even though it's only a few inches from the bathroom door, when you're locked in the bathroom with your foot stuck in the toilet.

The phone continued to ring as I waited, helplessly, counting the rings.

It was quite obvious to me now: I was totally alone in the house. Under any other circumstance, I would have been thrilled. Not now.

Eight . . . nine . . . ten . . . eleven rings. The phone stopped on the twelfth ring. *Just perfect,* I thought, disgusted with myself. *If only I'd closed the toilet lid before I crawled up here!*

If onlys always got me in trouble. I could easily get carried away with them. For example: *If only* Daddy's sister, Aunt Marla, hadn't died of cancer last year, leaving Uncle Jack sad and alone with four kids to raise. *If only* Daddy hadn't divorced Mom and moved to California. *If only* I'd hidden my diary key in a better place!

A giant cramp was beginning to zap my foot, creeping up my leg. Probably from the weird position I was standing in. Wait a minute! Why *was* I standing?

I decided to do myself a favor and sit down. It wasn't easy perched on the edge of the toilet seat. Pulling a towel off the rack, I rolled it up to make a softer, higher seat. It wasn't exactly comfortable, but it beat doing standing isometrics.

I was determined to look on the bright side of things. Let's see . . . something to be thankful for. I stared down into the toilet. Thank goodness, it was flushed!

Leaning my left arm against the sink, I was able to rest my head. Then I noticed the dripping faucet. I studied the situation, counting the seconds between drips. Every nine seconds a sizable droplet of water escaped from the faucet and fell into the sink. How many drops of water were lost each minute?

Hmm, I thought. *Sixty seconds in an hour. Nine into sixty is . . .*

"Got it!" I said out loud. "This faucet leaks 6.6 drops per minute." Wow! That was 396 drops per hour. What a waste.

Trickling water droplets tend to make people thirsty, so I reached for the paper cup holder beside the mirror.

"Holly!" a deep voice called from downstairs. "Are you up there?" It was Stan, the top-dog brousin in the Patterson-Meredith household.

"Help!" I yelled with all my might. "I'm stuck, er, locked in the bathroom."

I heard footsteps, welcoming them as my heart pounded.

"You're what?" Stan asked.

"I'm locked in the bathroom," I replied, standing up.

Oops! The towel slid into the toilet.

"Well, why don't you just turn the lock?" he said.

I shifted my balance. "I, uh, can't."

"Really?" Suspicion oozed from his vocal cords.

I waited, hoping he wouldn't leave me stranded. "It's kinda hard to explain. Uh, my foot's stuck!"

He chuckled. "What do you mean?"

I sighed. "If I tell you, promise you won't laugh?"

"Hey, this sounds good."

"Stan, do you *promise*?"

"Hey, whatever, girl."

I hated it when he said *girl* that way. It bugged me more than anything. My foot was killing me and so was my leg. "Promise me!" I demanded.

"What was the question again?"

"Stan!" Tears dripped off my face and onto the floor.

"Hey, calm down in there," he said. His voice grew suddenly gentle. "Are you hurt?"

"Not really hurt as in cut, slashed, or beaten. But bruised, now that's a major possibility," I answered.

Stan cleared his throat. "Where's your foot stuck, Holly?"

"In the toilet," I blurted.

Silence, total silence. And then I heard it, faintly at first—a ripple of laughter coming from the other side of the door.

"Stan, you promised!" I yelled, massaging the muscles in my thigh.

"Did not," he said, laughing harder than before.

"Look, I wouldn't be laughing if you were in this situation," I shouted over his cackling. But deep inside I knew I would be howling, too.

Finally he tried the door. "It's locked, all right. Now what do you want me to do?"

"Open the door, for starters," I demanded. "Take the door off the hinges." I hoped he'd move quickly. I was starting to feel a sharp pain in my foot, and strange muscle spasms fluttered up my leg.

"Good idea," he said. "I'll be right back."

Minutes ticked away like the slow drips emerging from the faucet. Three hundred ninety-six times, twenty-four hours a day. I wasn't even close to figuring the multiplication when I heard Stan's footsteps on the stairs.

Bang-a-whack! It sounded like he was hammering the hinges. "I'll have you outta there in a jiffy, little sister," he said in the worst John Wayne imitation of all time.

"Please hurry," I whispered prayerfully.

Br-r-ing! The phone rang again.

"Don't answer it," I shouted to Stan. "Get the door off first."

I could hear him grunting. Taking doors off hinges must be lots harder than it looks when they do it in the movies. The phone kept ringing. Was it Jared? Right now, I didn't care who was calling.

Six rings later, Stan heaved the door up and off the doorframe. He propped it against the banister in the hall and raced to the phone.

"Stan!" I turned on the whine the way Stephie does. "Come back."

I could hear Stan's voice just around the corner in the hallway. He was talking politely for a change. Then he said, "Please wait a second."

Suddenly he appeared, his head peeking into the bathroom. He gasped dramatically when he spied my foot in the toilet. "Man, you're not kidding," he said. Then he held up the portable phone. "It's your father. Long distance."

"I can't talk now," I snapped.

Stan shook his head. "I don't think that'll fly. He's leaving for an appointment in a few minutes. Says he wants to bounce an idea off you before he leaves the house."

"Fabulous," I whispered, accepting the phone from Stan.

"Hi, Holly-Heart," Daddy said, using the nickname Mom gave me because I was born on Valentine's Day.

"Hey. What's up?"

"It just occurred to me that you and Carrie have a long vacation from school coming up soon. I wanted to invite both of you here for Christmas." He exhaled into the phone. "What do you think?"

Think? How can you think with stabbing pain running up and down your leg? "Uh, Daddy, let me think about it and call you later. Okay?" I hoped he wouldn't misunderstand my abrupt response.

"That's fine, honey. Call me after seven tonight, your time. I believe I've caught you at a busy time."

Busy I could handle. Stuck in the toilet was a different matter. "I'll call you later, Daddy," I said, wincing as I handed the phone back to Stan.

"Looks like you're hurt," Stan said. "Let's get you outta there."

I tried to jerk my numb foot out of the toilet, but nothing happened. I wanted to scream.

Maybe they'd have to amputate. Or maybe I'd have to walk around with a toilet attached to my foot for the rest of my life. I guess there could be worse things. Maybe I could launch a sweeping fashion trend in Dressel Hills. Who needs elevator shoes when you can wear a toilet?

Stan looked at me funny. "Holly, you're not paying attention to anything I just said."

"I'm trying to divert my mind away from the pain."

"Can you wiggle your toes?" he asked.

"A little."

"Good." He leaned over and looked into the toilet. "What is that towel doing in there?"

"Keeping my foot company. What do you think?" And then an idea struck. "Quick, go get some dish detergent."

He stared at me. "What for?"

"Just get it," I said. There was no feeling left in my right foot. Maybe gangrene had set in. If the soap trick didn't work, maybe the paramedics would have to break the toilet with the Jaws of Life!

3

Stan returned with a bottle of lemon Joy in his hand.

I grabbed it from him and began to squeeze it upside down into the toilet. "Now, swish the soap around with your hands," I suggested.

He backed away. "You've gotta be kidding."

"We need lots of suds," I said seriously. "That's how Andie got a cheap ring off her finger once. The soap will make the toilet slippery. Trust me."

Stan opened the cabinet under the sink. He pulled out a toilet brush. "Here, try this."

First I used the end of the brush to dip the wet towel out of the toilet. With a fling, I tossed it into the bathtub. Then I stirred the brush around, faster and faster till it resembled a white tornado.

Like some miracle, the soap trick worked.

Slowly I eased my foot out of the tight opening. I wanted to dance for joy, but my foot was too sore. So I simply flushed the toilet.

Stan sat on the edge of the bathtub beside me as I unzipped my soaked boot. "I need an honest answer from you," he said, grinning from ear to ear.

"Ask me anything." I felt mighty giddy.

He scratched his blond head. "How does one's foot land in the toilet, anyhow?"

I wasn't about to reveal the reason for my afternoon's adventure. Not in a zillion years! "My lips are sealed," I said, patting his arm. "But thanks for the rescue attempt, brousin."

"No problem. Glad it was a success, little sister." There it was again, Stan's lousy John Wayne imitation. But it didn't matter; it was fabulous having this conversation with my new step-brother—the first decent one since the Patterson take-over.

Stan got up to leave. Suddenly he stopped and stared down at me. "Uh, Holly, are you really okay?"

"I think so, why?"

A very serious expression spread across his face. "You look a little *flushed*, that's all."

"Why you!" I screamed and tried to stand up. When I did, I lost my balance and toppled into the tub onto the wet towel. I decided right then and there I'd never, ever wear perfumed toilet water, no matter *who* gave it to me.

While Stan put the door back on its hinges, I soaked my aching foot in the tub with Epsom salts and warm water. As for the boot, it was hopeless. If I worked at it, I might have enough baby-sitting money saved up to buy another pair in a couple of months.

Then I remembered Daddy's long-distance phone call. Maybe the California Santa could bring me an exact duplicate on December twenty-fifth. I decided to call him back after supper. I wasn't exactly sure how Mom would take it, but I knew it would be fun to spend the holidays in a sunny beach setting.

Drying my foot with a clean towel, I thought about the advantages of wave surfing at Christmas as opposed to what we usually did at home—snow skiing. Surfing in December would make great headlines for my diary.

Oh yeah . . . the diary key, the reason for my slide into the toilet. Glancing up at the wicker cabinet above the toilet, I grinned. Perfect hiding place—even I couldn't get to it.

When I was finished drying my foot, I closed the toilet lid. Gingerly, I stepped up and planted my feet firmly on top. Reaching up, I lifted the flower arrangement and felt for the diary key underneath it. I leaned up on my tiptoes, my left foot—still wearing the dry boot—supporting me as I groped for the key. If only I could see what I was doing.

Inch by inch, my right hand covered the entire area while my left hand held the dried flower arrangement. Where *was* it? I felt around again. And again. It was useless. The key to my life's secrets had vanished!

I replaced the flower arrangement and did a one-footed hop off the toilet seat. I couldn't decide which was worse, being stuck in the toilet or losing the key. The whole thing was a nightmare—the absolute worst.

Back in my room, I spotted a note stuck to my mirror. In Carrie's handwriting it said, *I found your diary key in the bathroom yesterday. Here it is.* A tiny silver key was taped to the paper.

Wait till I get my hands on her, I thought, ripping the key off the paper and dropping it into my pocket. Boiling with anger, I opened the closet door and reached for my bathrobe.

Back in the bathroom, I turned the shower on full blast. I was certain that Carrie had helped herself to the pages of my diary. It wasn't the first time and probably wouldn't be the last. Not unless I came up with a better hiding place.

Soaping up, I envisioned the packing process for my trip to California. Along with clothes—and as many mystery novels as I could squeeze in—I would take a locked overnight case full of diaries, past and present. It was the perfect hiding place; in fact, it might be the only answer to my super-snooper problem at the moment. Why wait till California when a crawl space could serve the same purpose? Carrie and Stephie would never think to look under the steps for diaries—stashed away in a suitcase.

I couldn't wait to investigate the storage space under the family room steps. What genius!

After dressing, I went to my room to dry my hair. When someone knocked on the door, I switched the hair dryer off, ready to do battle for a little privacy. "If it's Carrie or Stephie, stay out," I called.

It was Stan. "Hey, you sound tough."

I opened the door to see him grinning in the hallway. "Jared awaits," he said, handing the portable phone to me.

I closed the door and snuggled into my canopy bed. "Hi, Jared," I said into the phone.

"How's Holly-Heart?"

Jared's smooth approach always took me off guard. I giggled a little.

"Miss you," he said softly. "Can't wait to see you at church tomorrow."

I ran my fingers through my hair, waiting for my heart to slow down. "We're going to early service," I told him.

"That's cool—one less hour till I see you."

Jared was pouring on the charm. Again. He'd already won me over last month by passing my scrutiny test—after Danny Myers and I decided to be just friends.

"You don't have to sweet-talk me anymore," I teased.

"I speak no other language around my Holly-Heart."

I laughed. "Talk normal, okay?" Really, sometimes Jared was too much! "So what are you doing?" I asked, propping my sore foot on a throw pillow.

"Checking on how you're doing with Miss W's latest writing assignment."

"The research part is fun," I said. "I'm doing my paper on the Sally Lightfoot crab. What're you doing?"

Jared paused. I heard him flipping pages. "Ready for this?"

I sighed. *What was he up to now?*

"Ever hear of the Goliath beetle of Nyassaland, Africa?" he asked seriously.

I couldn't help it; I laughed. Hard.

"What's so funny?" he said. "Don't you like my choice of insect?"

"It's fine," I said. "It's just, uh, I don't know . . ."

"What?"

"It sounds biblical, I guess."

"That's why I picked it," Jared insisted. "If there's a beetle called Goliath, where's that put David?"

I giggled so hard, I snorted. "You're crazy."

"About *you*," he said.

I blushed. It was amazing, this transformation that had taken place in the past few months. Jared was totally different. He never flirted with other girls. Only with me.

"Holly? You still with me?" he asked. It was a double meaning.

In my heart I wanted to say *Yes, forever and always*, but I mumbled something about having to clean my room. I knew Mom and Uncle Jack wouldn't want me to get carried away with talking to Jared.

"I'll see you at church," he said. "Bye."

I said, "Good-bye, Jared," like the whole world rested on my phone farewell. But that's how things felt now between Jared and me.

At last, I'd found true puppy love . . . as Mom would say.

4

I began cleaning my third of the room. It was hopelessly messy with Stephie's stuffed animals strewn everywhere and Carrie's dirty clothes in a pile the size of Mount Everest. Well, almost. I stripped my bed and stuffed the sheets into a pillow slip. Then I heard Carrie and Stephie come in the front door downstairs.

Snatching the diary key out of my jeans pocket, I dashed down the steps, taking two at a time, even though my right foot still hurt a little from the toilet adventure.

I cornered the culprits in the living room. "You two better think long and hard about this," I said, waving the key in their faces. "This is off limits to you, and you know it."

Stephie's eyes grew wide. "I didn't do it," she shrieked. "I'm too short to reach that high."

Now I knew it was Stephie who'd spied on

me. "You just gave yourself away, little rascal," I said.

Then, turning to Carrie, I confronted her. "Stephie spies and you do the dirty work, is that it?"

Carrie stared at me in silence.

"You never used to do this stuff before Stephie moved in," I persisted. "Are you gonna let a seven-year-old control your brain?"

Carrie put her hands on her hips. "I don't have to listen to you, meanie," she said haughtily.

I flipped my damp hair over my shoulder and sat down. "Just wait'll Mom hears about your snooping. Now, sit down!"

Stephie folded her arms stubbornly. "Don't tell us what to do."

Still standing in the middle of the living room, Carrie snorted at me. Stephie mimicked Carrie's hands-on-hips routine.

I wanted to strangle them both, but fortunately Mom and Uncle Jack arrived. They looked tired from shopping. Uncle Jack smoothed his wind-blown hair, then helped Mom out of her coat and hung it in the closet.

"Mommy . . . hi!" Carrie hugged her.

Uncle Jack scooped Stephie up in his arms. He eyed me sitting on the sofa. "Looks like Judgment Day," he said, smiling at me.

I pointed to the girls. "And those are the accused."

Mom touched her soft, blond waves and sat beside me. "*Now* what?"

My side of the story was scarcely out when Stephie interrupted. "She's bossing us, Daddy. We can't do anything right around here."

"How about starting with a little respect for privacy?" I suggested.

I could tell Carrie knew where this conversation was headed. She started making jerky cutthroat signs with her pointer finger when Mom wasn't watching. My sister would be in big trouble if I started to spell things out.

"This house is too crowded," Stephie whined.

"Yeah," Carrie piped up. "We need more room."

"Your mother and I *have* discussed the possibility of adding on to the back of the house," Uncle Jack said.

Mom looked at each of us. "What do you think, girls?"

"Fabulous!" I said.

"When can we start?" Carrie asked.

"Immediately, as far as I'm concerned," Uncle Jack said, studying the Psalms calendar on the lamp table. "Let's see, if we get going on it next week, we can make some good progress by

Holly's birthday. What do you say, hon?"

It wasn't a question of money now that Uncle Jack was in the family. And with Mom working three days a week at the law firm doing paralegal work, there was probably plenty of extra money for things like this.

Mom nodded her head in agreement. I wanted to dance for joy. What a fabulous idea; I'd finally get my room back, along with my privacy!

Uncle Jack swung Stephie around. "The problem of overcrowding will be solved," he announced with a hearty chuckle.

"Yeah, but what about until the addition is built?" I asked. "Can't we make some stiffer laws for snoopers while the three of us are still stuck in the same room?"

"You bet we can," Uncle Jack said with a twinkle in his eyes. "And these laws *will* be enforced." He looked first at Carrie, then at Stephie as he made his point.

Yes! Finally I had the parental support I needed.

Mom pulled Carrie and Stephie over to her. "If either of you get into Holly's personal things, including her diary, there will be no TV for you for a full week."

"And double kitchen duty," Uncle Jack added.

Carrie and Stephie groaned as Mom and Uncle Jack went upstairs.

This was so fabulous I couldn't contain my excitement. I ran to the kitchen and ate a whole bowl of strawberry ice cream in nothing flat.

As I was finishing the last spoonful, Mom came downstairs and slid onto the bar stool next to me. "I understand your father called this morning." It was more of a question than a statement. "Stan left a note upstairs in our bedroom with a list of calls," she explained.

I sensed what was coming. She probably even suspected Daddy's personal invitation. "Well, I couldn't talk very long," I said. "I told him I'd call back tonight, if that's okay with you."

I paused, unsure how she'd take this news. "Daddy invited Carrie and me for Christmas." I avoided looking at her as I carried my ice-cream bowl to the sink. "What do you think?"

"As long as we have time to celebrate together here after you get back, it's okay with me," she said. "Besides, it might be the ideal time for you girls to go. Things could get chaotic with the extra rooms being built on to the back of the house." She stretched her arms, yawning.

I leaned my elbows on the bar. "Do you want to talk to Carrie about this or should I?" I remembered the last time Carrie was scheduled to visit Daddy. Last summer. She'd backed out at the last minute, so I went without her.

"I'll talk to her," Mom said, going over to the freezer. She reached for a family-size package of hamburger meat and placed it on the counter to thaw. Everything around here came in large quantities these days.

I sneaked up and squeezed her around the waist. "Sure you'll be all right spending Christmas alone with Uncle Jack and his kids?"

I giggled, knowing full well she'd have a fabulous time. Uncle Jack treated Mom like royalty. And even though everyone said they were in their honeymoon stage, I fully expected them to keep on being this happy. They were a perfect match. Uncle Jack and his hilarious humor, and Mom with her sweet qualities of kindness and patience. Made me want to be just like her, and maybe even marry a crazy guy like Uncle Jack someday.

As for Daddy, he was way too serious. Maybe I could get him to lighten up this Christmas. Besides that, maybe I could share with him the true reason for the season.

I headed downstairs to the crawl space to search for an overnight case. Suitcases of every size and shape were stashed back in the corner. Uncle Jack was a world traveler, and his collection of luggage proved it.

Blocking the path to the suitcases was a large

box of Christmas wrapping paper and ribbons. Seeing it gave me an idea. Two weeks from now, before school let out for the holidays, I would present my gift to Jared *and* to my secret pal. Last Sunday, the kids in our church youth group had drawn names. Mine was Paula Miller, but I'd traded with Billy Hill, who had Jared's name and wanted a girl instead. He was thrilled to get Paula's name from me.

I loved having Jared for my secret pal. It was so much fun to hide little notes and do special things when your secret pal was also your *guy* friend, too.

I picked up one of the rolls of brightly colored wrap and decided to use it to decorate my gift for Jared. Now . . . what to buy for him?

The cool suede boots hovered in the back of my mind. If I skipped buying another pair, I could afford something really special for Jared. If I could just buy one shoe—the *right* shoe—I'd be set. The left one was perfectly fine.

With that thought, I pushed the box of wrappings and ribbons aside and headed for the suitcases. Just as I reached for the white overnight case, I heard someone behind me. I spun around to see the tail end of Carrie's long hair flying.

"Not again," I whispered. Then I realized if I acted cool, she'd never suspect my secret plan. It was perfect!

5

After supper I called my dad in California.

"Meredith residence," he answered.

"It's Holly," I said. "Guess what? Carrie and I have decided to come for Christmas."

"That's wonderful news. Now, let's see, when is school out?" he asked.

"We go till Friday, the seventeenth," I explained, glancing at the calendar in the family room. "But Mom wants us back home before New Year's Eve—we're having our Christmas together then."

"That's great! You girls will be here for nearly two full weeks," Daddy said. "That'll give us plenty of time for a visit to Sea World and maybe a quick trip to Disneyland. It will be crowded, but I understand it's worth fighting the masses to see the Christmas parade."

"You've never seen the electric parade?" I asked, surprised.

"Too busy to take off, I guess," he replied.

I couldn't believe it. If I lived that close to L.A., I would want to see the Christmas festivities at Disneyland *every* year. That's the difference between my dad and me. He's all work and very little play. It was a good thing Carrie and I were spending Christmas with him this year. Maybe we could keep him from working such long hours.

"Holly, do you know what Carrie would like for Christmas?" Daddy asked.

"Ask her to write a list," I suggested. "I know she'll have lots of ideas for you."

He paused. "And what about you, Holly-Heart? Is there something special you want?"

I thought a moment about asking for a new pair of boots like the one I'd ruined in the toilet, but I changed my mind. "Whatever you get will be fine."

I was reluctant to ask for anything. After almost five years without him, just talking to him on the phone and visiting him occasionally was a gift in itself. But there *was* something I was dying to have. It was the heart locket Daddy had given Mom thirteen years ago on Valentine's Day—the day I was born. Somehow, when Daddy moved out, the locket had been packed with his things by mistake. Mom hadn't minded that much, maybe because of their divorce. But I did. Anyway, there was no way I could gather the courage to mention it to Daddy. Only my diary recorded my true feelings about the necklace.

His voice interrupted my thoughts. "Is Carrie available? I'd like to speak to her."

"Sure, I'll get her. Just a minute." I called for Carrie. Twice. At last she came running downstairs.

"What'll I say to him?" she whispered when I told her who it was.

"Let Daddy do the talking," I advised.

She pushed her long golden locks behind her left shoulder. "Hello?" she said shyly.

I watched Carrie as she talked to Daddy. She hardly knew him. Daddy and Mom had separated when she was only four years old. It was hard for *me* to remember much about the divorce, and I had been eight when it happened.

Carrie started naming off gift options for herself. She started with brand-name dolls, then listed book titles and computer software.

"Enough," I whispered, motioning to her. I didn't want her to sound like a greedy little brat.

Shortly, she handed the phone back to me. "Here, he wants to talk to you." Carrie scampered back upstairs.

"Hi, again," I said into the phone.

"I'll send the tickets well before your flight," Daddy said. "Do you want to fly out Friday night or wait till Saturday morning?"

I wouldn't think of missing the youth group party Friday night for anything! But I was hesitant to tell Daddy about it. He might think my social life was more important than spending the extra day with him. "Uh, we'll fly out on Saturday if that's okay," I said.

"I might have a business lunch that day, though I don't know for sure," he said. "If so, I'll have Saundra pick you girls up at the airport."

I wanted to beg him not to send our stepmom, but I bit my tongue. Surely Daddy would leave his lunch meeting early enough to come for us himself.

"Well, I guess that's it for now," he said. "Oh yes, Tyler says hi. He's looking forward to meeting Carrie, and he's eager to see you again, Holly."

I remembered the nine-year-old boy—our stepbrother—who lived in my father's house on the beach. Tyler was one of the best reasons to visit my dad and his new wife. Last summer when I visited, Tyler and I had made a fabulous sand castle.

Saying good-bye to Daddy, I thought about the castle on the beach. Tyler and I had designed

a blueprint on paper before we ever started building. It had taken three hours, but our Castle
Royale was magnificent, complete with tiny
toothpick flags, tinfoil windows, and Popsicle
stick balconies. A true work of art!

Tyler had marched around the castle like a
soldier on guard duty. He said he was in charge
of his creation. That's when I told him the story
of our beginnings. Adam and Eve. It was hard to
believe, but Tyler had never heard the Genesis
story. Here was a kid growing up in a posh beach
house on the West Coast, and he'd totally missed
the creation account in the Bible! Tyler and I
talked for a long time about it. It was strange discussing things like that with a kid. But Tyler
wasn't just any boy. He was very bright, and I
looked forward to seeing him again.

Tyler's mother, Saundra, was another story.
There was something about her that made me
want to turn and run. Maybe it was that bright
red lipstick of hers—I never saw her without it
the whole time I was there! Maybe it was the
way things had to be absolutely perfect around
her. Not just her makeup and hair, but everything, right down to the cloth napkins on the
table at *breakfast!* I felt sorry for Daddy. Why had
he chosen someone so different from Mom?

These were just a few of the many questions
that continued to haunt me about Daddy and his

new life. But . . . The Question, the one buried deep inside my heart, was so mixed up with the pain of lost years, I was sure I could never bring myself to ask it.

6

It was two days before the Christmas party. I got up extra early and packed my backpack with textbooks, notebooks, and . . . yes, my diary. Lately I'd been taking it to school and writing in it during study hall, far away from the eyes of super snoopers.

I pulled a pen out of my bag, then tiptoed to the bathroom, letting Carrie and Stephie sleep. I felt my diary key dangling on the chain under my nightshirt. Wearing it was the only way to secure the greatest secrets of my life.

I'd changed my mind about hiding the diary in an overnight case. It was too inconvenient, for one thing, and I didn't trust Carrie not to look in the crawl space. I was convinced she'd go to great lengths to keep up with the ongoing happenings between Jared Wilkins and me. So I changed my tactics. I began sleeping with my diary.

The idea had come from a dream I had. Not only was my diary beside me in bed, it was tied to my wrist with a sound alarm cued for activation by the slightest tug on the string. It worked well in the dream, but in reality I simply tied the diary to my wrist. I wasn't smart enough to wire it for sound.

In the bathroom I lowered the toilet lid and sat on it to write in my diary.

Wednesday, December 15. I can't wait to see Jared's expression when I give him my Christmas gift. It's fabulous! I bought a cool cloth-covered book with blank pages at Explore Bookstore yesterday. It cost a little over twelve dollars with tax. (Borrowed from Stan till later.)

Today I'll transfer the poems from my diary to the new book during study hall. I'm calling it, "A Heart Full of Poetry: At Christmas."

I keep wondering who Jared's secret pal is. He's keeping it a secret from everyone. Another big question is: What will he give me for Christmas? Even though he hasn't mentioned it, I'm sure he'll surprise me with something. It's going to be so exciting when we exchange gifts at Pastor Rob's house on Friday. There's a huge redwood deck off the kitchen with a great view of the mountains. Maybe Jared and I can give our gifts to each other outside on the deck, by ourselves. I'd prefer that.

I closed the diary, locked it, and put the

chain around my neck. Stashing my diary in my backpack, I undressed and hopped into the shower.

♥   ♥   ♥

At school, my best friend, Andie, was waiting at my locker. "Where have you been?" she demanded breathlessly.

I glanced at my watch. "Am I late?"

"No, but I have to talk to you." She pulled me down the hall and into the girls' rest room.

I leaned my backpack on the edge of the sink. "What's going on?"

"Paula Miller's up to something," she whispered, checking under all the stalls—looking for feet, no doubt. "I ran into her downtown after school yesterday."

I peered into the mirror, checking my hair. "What's so earthshaking about that?"

Andie continued, her dark eyes flashing. "Paula said she was buying a Christmas present for her secret pal."

I hadn't the faintest clue where Andie was going with this. "Get to the point," I said, looking at my watch. Seven minutes to first period.

"Just listen," she said. "This morning I saw

Paula hiding a Christmas present in her locker. I sneaked up behind her locker, and guess what I saw?"

Andie was dying to inform me; I could tell by the pre-explosive look on her face. "So, tell me," I said, playing along.

Andie grabbed my arm. "Holly, brace yourself. The tag on Paula's gift said, *To Jared W.*" She sighed. "Do you still want to rush off to first period?"

I was burning-up mad. "Jared's *my* secret pal!" I shouted. "What's she trying to prove?"

"Beats me," Andie muttered. "Maybe she's faking it—like she drew his name or something. Might just be her latest attempt to win points with him."

I shoved my hair over my shoulder. "Won't she freak when she finds out who really drew Jared's name?"

Andie turned and looked in the mirror, touching her dark, layered curls. "Jared's not dense. He'll figure it out when you give him your gift at the party." Andie's smile gave way to a grin. I could tell she was enjoying this strange turn of events. I, on the other hand, was dying to know why Paula Miller was launching another attention-getting campaign at Jared!

"I can't believe she'd do that," I said as we rushed to our lockers. "Paula's gotta be out of her mind to mess with Jared. He won't bite—not after the scrutiny test I put him through last month."

Unless . . . Was something going on between them I didn't know about?

My fears began to diminish when I saw Jared waiting at my locker. "Hey, you look fabulous," he said, using my word. "Ready for the party?"

"Can't wait." I dropped off the books I didn't need and slammed the locker door.

He leaned over and whispered, "Me too." He flashed that adorable grin of his and offered to carry my books.

"You'll be late to class," I protested. But he reached for them anyway, walking me to science, then darted off to beat the bell.

Excited, I hurried in to find my assigned seat. Jared was adorable, and we were going to the Christmas party together. None of Paula Miller's foolish plans could change that!

Mr. Ross stepped up to the podium, beginning his lecture on molecules. I tried to listen, but my mind kept wandering back to Andie's latest sleuthing efforts. What was Paula thinking, buying a present for Jared and passing it off as a secret-pal gift? And why would she risk bringing it to school, when someone like Andie was sure to see?

Hurrah for Andie, the truest friend ever—

always looking out for me. Maybe she would keep an eye on Paula while I was in California visiting Daddy. Who knows what that girl might pull with Jared left here all alone.

I yanked my three-ring binder out of my backpack and began to take notes, scribbling to keep up with Mr. Ross. His lectures reminded me of a hundred-yard dash. He spoke in spurts, leaning on his wooden podium. Then he took a long breath and traipsed around his desk before he began lecturing again—faster than ever. At least I didn't have to stare at his smudged glasses anymore. Ever since he started dating Miss Wannamaker, my creative writing teacher, he'd replaced his glasses with contacts. A sure sign of love.

After science, Jared rushed over to me in the hall. "Holly-Heart, what color are you wearing Friday night?"

"Probably pink," I said, my cheeks growing warm.

"Your favorite color, right?" he said.

I nodded. What was Jared up to? I imagined him presenting me with a pink corsage. "Wait," I said, changing my mind. "Maybe I'll wear red, you know, for Christmas."

Jared shrugged his shoulders. "Well, which is it?" he teased.

"Poinsettia pink," I said, laughing.

"What's that?"

"It's sorta dusty, you know, a cross between a rose color and . . ."

Just then Paula Miller bumped into Jared. Her books went flying, with a little too much assistance on her part. Jared stooped down to pick them up, and as he did, Paula leaned over and asked him to meet her after lunch. Honestly, she didn't *speak* her request. It was a definite purr. And right in front of me! She was flirting with Jared!

I wanted to storm off to my next class, but I stayed put beside Jared, waiting for his response.

Jared merely nodded. "I'll see you at your locker," he said, like it was no big deal. But it was to *me*, and I was determined to find out what was going on.

♥　　♥　　♥

At lunch Jared and I sat together as usual. Danny Myers joined us later, listening as I told Jared about my Christmas plans.

"So you're going to California for Christmas," Danny said, like he was very interested.

I swallowed a bite of hot dog and reached for a napkin. "My dad's flying Carrie and me out."

He took a drink of hot tea. Probably the

decaffeinated, herbal kind. "Don't forget who your friends are," he said seriously.

"Don't worry." I glanced at Jared. "It'll be fun—at least for a little while."

Jared leaned his shoulder next to mine. "It'll be fun for Holly, but . . ." and here he broke into song, "I'll have a blue, blue Christmas without her."

Danny chuckled. But his beaming eyes made me a tad suspicious. Was he happy for me because Jared and I were finally getting along? Or did he miss me?

"Well, I hate to leave you two alone like this," Jared kidded, "but I have to meet someone before my next class."

I swallowed hard, wishing Jared had forgotten about his prearranged meeting with Paula.

"See you after school, Holly-Heart," he said, winking.

My heart fluttered only slightly. Why was he running off to meet her? I was jittery inside, wishing I could hurry out and spy on Jared. It bugged me sitting here making small talk with Danny.

Finally, when I could stand it no longer, I made my move. "I've gotta run," I said, excusing myself.

"No problem," Danny said with a smile. "See you Friday at the party?"

"Yep." I waved good-bye to him.

When I had deposited my tray, I noticed Danny's table was suddenly surrounded by Kayla Miller—Paula's twin—and two other girls. It made me feel a little better to know I wasn't leaving Danny by himself. Now, on to spy on Jared's locker rendezvous with Paula.

I dashed down the hall, past the main office. Hiding behind an open classroom door, I scanned the row of lockers. There they were, in front of Paula's locker. Jared's back was turned to me—thank goodness! Paula smiled up at Jared, flashing her perfect white teeth. She gestured as she spoke, and fluffed her hair flirtatiously.

I was boiling inside. How rude! Who did she think she was?

Paula reached up and took the gift out of her locker. It was lavishly wrapped with shiny striped paper and topped with a large green-and-white bow.

No way would Jared accept her gift. Not unless she actually lied about it. Maybe she was giving it to him early to trick him into thinking she had drawn his name. Desperately I tried to second-guess her plan. This was too weird!

Along with being angry, I was secretly amused. How would Paula react if Jared refused her gift? I was dying to know. After his refusal,

Jared would set Paula straight about us. What a scene that would be.

I longed to hear their conversation. Paula held up the fancy gift, playing with the ribbon on the top, chattering incessantly. Inching closer, I noticed Jared turn slightly and glance at his watch. Yes! Just as I thought. He was going to leave her standing in the dust.

Then an incredible thing happened. Paula whispered something in Jared's ear. Then she held the gift out, and Jared actually accepted it.

Strains of Christmas music began to flutter through the hall from the school office. Someone was playing "I'll Be Home for Christmas." Probably the school secretary. The sentimental melody washed over me as Jared waved to Paula.

I wanted to cry. Instead, I turned and fled, searching frantically for my best friend.

7

I found Andie in study hall working on last-minute math homework. "I have to talk to you," I whispered, settling into the desk in front of hers. Then I spilled out the events I had just witnessed.

She stuck her pencil in her math book and closed it. "Holly, your relationship with Jared is at stake," she said, as if I didn't already know. "Listen to me, and do exactly what I tell you."

"Okay, like what?"

She twirled a strand of hair around her finger. Trouble was brewing! "Prissy Paula has had her eyes on Jared ever since she and her twin sister moved to Dressel Hills. Here's what you do—totally ignore her."

"But how can I? She's everywhere!"

Andie's lips spread into a forced grin. "Pretend she doesn't exist."

"And then what?" I asked, dumbfounded at this ridiculous idea.

"If you act mature about the whole thing, Jared will be so impressed he'll start ignoring Paula, too."

"I, uh, don't know about this."

Andie nodded her head slowly. "Paula's trying to make you mad. I think that's part of what's motivating her." She crossed her arms deliberately and leaned on the desk. "She probably thinks you'll confront Jared about this, and that could blow your relationship with him."

"Really . . . you think so?"

"You betcha." Suddenly she looked serious. "Nobody likes to be cornered, least of all Jared. It's part of the game." She picked up her pencil.

"Andie, you're incredible!"

She relished the compliment. I could tell by the way she sat there grinning, her brown eyes sparkling.

Deep inside, I wondered about Jared. Why would he accept a Christmas gift from Paula unless she really did lie about getting his name? And if not, had he been fooling me all these weeks?

"For now," Andie added quietly, "be cool and see what happens at the party."

I rummaged through my bag and found my locked diary. It was time to transfer my *Heart Full of Poetry* to the red-and-green-plaid covered book—for Jared. As I copied the first poem in my best handwriting, I thought about my relationship with Jared Wilkins. True, we'd had a parade of ups and downs, but I thought things were settled between us. I *wanted* to trust him. And only something like this thing with Paula could make me doubt him.

🖤   🖤   🖤

I ran to catch the city bus after school. If I hurried, I could get home before the snoopers invaded my territory. I needed some privacy while I wrapped Jared's gift.

After hopping off the bus, I heard loud hammering coming from halfway down the street. I paused to listen. It was coming from behind my house. Thanks to a lack of normally heavy snows, our two-room addition was coming along nicely.

Inside the house, I hurried to the crawl space, my backpack still slung over my shoulder. Spotting the box overflowing with Christmas wrap and ribbons, I chose the prettiest paper I could find and a bright red bow to match. I hurried to my room.

Bam! Bam! The hammering continued.

Upstairs I found Carrie and Stephie building something out of Legos that resembled a spaceship.

"What are you two doing home?" I asked.

"Early dismissal," Carrie said.

I looked at the Lego chaos everywhere. "This room is a massive mess!"

"Don't worry, we'll clean it up," Carrie said absentmindedly.

"Do it now," I said.

The girls looked up at me. "We were here first," Stephie said.

I closed the door. Stephie was wrong again; *I* was here first! Her snide remark echoed in my brain to the beat of the hammering outside. "Sassy little girl," I muttered, hurrying to the kitchen for some tape and a scissors. "I was born first, inhabited that room first, and . . ."

"Hey, Holly, you're talking to yourself again," Stan said, coming in the back door.

"Trying for some sanity," I said, hoping he'd make himself scarce and leave me alone to wrap my present in peace.

"Hungry?" he asked. He tossed his jacket on the counter beside my Christmas wrap.

I sighed.

"Not talking to me today?" He made a beeline to the refrigerator. "How about a sandwich?"

Bam! Bam! The pounding was getting to me. Really getting to me.

"Turkey and cheese okay?" he yelled over the noise, holding the refrigerator door open, waiting for my response.

"No mustard, please," I mumbled.

"Man, something's really got to you." Stan poured a glass of milk.

I didn't dare tell him what was bugging me. He might mention it to Billy Hill, or worse, Danny Myers, and it would get back to Jared. I was determined to stick with Andie's plan and pretend Paula and Jared had never met today at her locker.

I thanked Stan when he presented a sandwich to me on a napkin. Then he disappeared down the stairs to the family room-turned-bedroom.

Must be nice having the largest room in the house, I thought.

I was struggling with that old familiar feeling—jealousy. And I was dealing with it on more than one level these days. But Stan and his cozy retreat downstairs were easier to handle than Paula and her sneaky tactics.

I grabbed three grapes and popped them into my mouth as I reached for the dishcloth. Draping Stan's jacket over a stool, I wiped the top of the bar. Next, I dried the area, then began to unroll the wrapping paper, eager to make Jared's gift as dazzling as possible. No question, it would be better than Paula's any day.

Once the poetry book was neatly wrapped, I carried my school bag upstairs to the communal bedroom. I decided not to comment again on the Lego disaster as I tiptoed around the maze of tiny pieces to the closet. On days like this, I'd have given my right arm for a walk-in closet. Privacy was more important than ever, now that I had none at all.

Searching through my end of the closet, I found the rosy-pink blouse I had described to Jared. It would look fabulous with my new black pants. I whisked the blouse out of the closet and grabbed my backpack, heading for Mom's bedroom.

Closing the door, I posed in Mom's tall mirror behind the door. I held the silky blouse under my neck, staring at my reflection. If everything went well, the party was going to be so perfect. A night to remember.

Just then I heard the mail truck pull up. Peeking through the lace curtains, I saw the mail carrier climb out of the white truck and head up the walk toward the house.

I dropped my backpack and laid the blouse on Mom's bed. I ran downstairs, arriving at the door just as the postman rang the bell.

"Here you are, Missy." He held out a stack of mail. One was marked Express Mail.

"Thanks," I said, eager to open the large white envelope with my name on it. I ran to the kitchen, grabbed the letter opener out of the drawer, and sliced into the envelope.

Inside, I found two sets of airplane tickets. One for Carrie, and one for me. And there was a letter from Daddy. I began to read.

> *Dear Holly,*
> *You and Carrie are booked to leave this Friday night at nine-thirty.*

"Oh no, he's got it all wrong," I whispered, my heart pounding.

> *I realize you preferred to leave Saturday, but holiday schedules are tight, so I took what my travel agent could arrange. Hopefully this won't cause any hardship on your end.*
> *We'll see you in two days.*
Love, Daddy

"Hardship? This is horrible!" I shouted, punching the air. "How could he mess up like this?"

Carrie and Stephie came galloping downstairs. Stephie dragged my backpack behind her.

"Give me that," I said, snatching it from her. Heading upstairs, I stopped in my tracks, remembering there was no privacy to be had in my bedroom. In fact, there was none anywhere in this house.

Furious about my dad's mistake, I grabbed my jacket and fumbled to put it on. Then I dashed outside—behind the house—barging into the middle of the unfinished addition. The workers stopped their hammering and stared at me as I knelt down on the cold cement foundation and crumpled Daddy's letter. I didn't care what they thought. My estranged father had just ruined my entire Christmas—and maybe my life!

8

"Why is this happening to me?" I sobbed into the phone hours later, telling Andie my sad tale.

She was doing her best to calm me down. "Hang on a minute, Holly. You can still go to the party. Just pack your stuff ahead of time and ask your mom to pick you up at Pastor Rob's. You can leave for the airport from there."

"That's easy for you to say," I said, sniffling. "Your guy's not accepting gifts from gorgeous brunettes."

"I thought we had that problem settled," she scolded.

I sighed loudly. "Maybe *you* did."

"So what are you gonna do, Holly? Confront Jared, make him mad, and lose him in time for Christmas?"

Andie was right, as usual.

I blew my nose. "Okay, I'll try it your way."

"Look, I've gotta run," Andie said abruptly. "Mom needs me."

"Okay," I said reluctantly, hearing the sounds of Andie's two-year-old twin brothers in the background. "Hey, thanks, Andie," I added. "You're a good friend."

"Don't you forget it." With that, she hung up.

I ran upstairs to survey my wardrobe for California before Mom and Uncle Jack arrived home. It was going to be tight, but I intended to get Carrie's and my clothes washed and packed in time to head for the airport directly from the party.

Mom was agreeable when I mentioned it. "You don't have to convince me of the importance of this church event, Holly-Heart," she said, touching my head. "I know."

I leaned against the sink, watching her chop lettuce for the salad. "Thanks, Mom." I hugged her. "I'm going to miss you."

She put the knife down and dried her hands. Then she wrapped her arms around me. "You're my sweetie, you know that, don't you?"

I nodded, blinking back the tears. It wasn't going to be easy leaving her. It would be my very first Christmas away from her—and Dressel Hills.

"It'll be nice coming home to my old room," I said, wiping my face.

Mom motioned for me to sit at the bar. She scooted onto the stool across from me. "Your uncle Jack thinks a lot of you, Holly-Heart. The addition we're having built isn't just to make more bedroom space for his kids. It's much more than that."

"I think I know what you're saying. It's Uncle Jack's way of showing how much he cares about *your* kids, too, right?"

Mom nodded, smiling. "Jack's a wonderful man. I'm truly blessed to be his wife." I could tell she meant it by the way her blue eyes twinkled as she spoke his name.

♥   ♥   ♥

With Mom's help, I was packed and ready long before the party. Uncle Jack let Stan drive the van to Pastor Rob's house. Mom stayed home with the rest of the kids until it was time to head for the airport.

I sat behind Stan in the van, watching his every move. He was turning out to be less of a jerk than I'd ever imagined. And responsible. He checked the intersection of Aspen Street and Downhill Court twice before accelerating.

"You're doing fine, son," Uncle Jack said,

casting a quick wink at me. "It won't be long and we'll be giving Holly driving lessons."

"Yeah, in less than two years I'll have my permit," I said. Funny, I felt more confident about learning to drive than about seeing Paula in the same room with Jared.

"And if you're too busy, maybe I can teach her," Stan said, glancing into the rearview mirror. Our eyes locked for an instant. Stan wasn't kidding; he was really on my side.

When we pulled into the driveway, Stan turned off the ignition, handing the keys to his dad. He picked up the present for his secret pal and turned around in the driver's seat. "Hope you have fun in the sun, Holly."

"I'll try," I said, holding my gift for Jared.

"Let me know if you run out of money," Stan said. "I charge twenty-five percent interest." He was joking, but I didn't mind. It was his way of saying he'd miss me. He leaped out of the driver's seat, heading for the party.

"Watch out for suntanned beach bums," Uncle Jack teased as I climbed out of the van. "Don't go California crazy."

"Don't worry," I said, thinking of my one and only crush. No way would I fall for some tall, tan surfer with Jared Wilkins waiting for me back home. I waved to Uncle Jack once more.

Inside, the house was bustling with zillions of

kids. Pastor Rob greeted me and took my jacket. A tall Christmas tree stood in the middle of the window at one end of the room. It was decorated with red and white velvet bows and homemade ornaments. I hid Jared's gift among the many secret-pal presents under the tree.

At the other end of the room, a crowd of kids gathered around a grand piano. Andie was playing "Jingle Bell Rock," while Stan leaned on the piano, grinning at her. Joy and Amy-Liz tossed popcorn into Andie's mouth as her fingers flew over the keys.

When Joy saw me, she rushed over. "Merry Christmas, Holly," she said, pushing a small gift into my hands. "I'm your secret pal," she whispered.

"You are?" I said, pulling tape off the side. "I never would've guessed." A white box peeked out of the wrapping. I tugged on it and opened the lid. Inside, nestled on the cotton lining, was a black velvet choker with a cross hanging from a gold chain. "Ooh," I whispered, and gave her a hug. "I love it. Thanks!"

"Who's *your* secret pal?" she asked, her eyes bright with anticipation.

"I'm not telling yet," I said, looking around for Jared. And Paula.

"Oh, in case you wondered, Jared's in the kitchen pulling taffy with Billy Hill," Joy said, heading back to the piano, where Andie was accumulating admirers and carolers.

"Where's Shauna?" I asked, following Joy to the piano. Shauna and Joy were inseparable friends.

"She has the flu," Joy said. "She's missed out on everything all week."

"That's too bad," I said, watching Andie's chubby fingers bounce around the octaves in the bass. "Tell her I missed her tonight, okay?"

Joy nodded and smiled.

Andie stopped playing long enough to slide over on the bench. "Let's sing 'Carol of the Bells,' " she suggested, patting the bench.

I sat beside her, glancing around at the eligible vocalists. "Let's make it a round," I said.

"Good idea," Stan agreed. "But some of us need the music."

Andie rolled an arpeggio up the keyboard, holding the broken chord with the pedal. "I don't." She flashed a flirtatious smile at Stan.

"Look out," Joy teased. "Andie's playing by ear again."

Stan laughed and reached for the songbook. Scanning the index, his finger ran down the page. "Found it," he said, holding the book open for Andie.

After another introductory flourish by Andie, the guys began to sing. Joy, Amy-Liz, and I came in with the repeated melody, creating a two-part harmony. Soon, Kayla and several other girls from the kitchen joined in.

Where was Paula?

At the end of our fabulous rendition, we clapped and hooted. This was going to be the best Christmas party ever!

I hurried upstairs to put my gift from Joy on the lamp table in one of the bedrooms. There, a mountain of jackets was piled on the bed. Back downstairs, I peeked into the kitchen and saw Billy and Jared pulling taffy. Pastor Rob was supervising.

"Come help us, Holly," Billy called, motioning with his head.

Jared looked up just then; his face burst into a grin. "There she is," he announced to everyone. That's when I noticed Jared's shirt. It matched my rosy-pink blouse!

I hurried to his side. "So that's why you asked what color I was wearing," I whispered.

He nodded, his arms stretched out in front of him. "Here, someone take my place." He pulled his fingers away from the sticky taffy. Then, out of the crowded kitchen, Paula Miller emerged.

She picked up the taffy marked with Jared's fingerprints and flashed her Colgate smile at me as Jared washed his hands at the sink.

Was I ever glad I'd traded names with Billy

for the secret-pal gift exchange. I couldn't imagine buying a present for pathetic Paula.

Jared and I headed into the living room. We sang several more Christmas carols and helped string popcorn on the tree.

"I have a surprise for you," I said during a semi-quiet moment. "Let's go out on the deck for a minute, okay?"

Jared followed me to the Christmas tree and waited while I found his present. He held the patio door for me as we walked into the frosty night.

It was colder than I'd expected, but the view was fabulous, just the way I'd imagined it would be. We leaned on the redwood railing, gazing at the mountains, black against the moonlit sky. Pungent smells of woodsmoke enhanced the atmosphere. Perfect!

I held up my gift to Jared. "Merry Christmas! I'm your secret pal."

He looked surprised. "Really? *You* are?"

I nodded, shivering in the wintry stillness. "This present isn't for just *any* secret pal, you know."

Jared grinned down at me. Suddenly the light on the deck flashed on. We turned to see the faces of our friends pressed against the kitchen window. Paula was among the kids waving and laughing as the light blinked on and off, on and off.

"Not her again," I muttered.

"What did you say?" Jared leaned his ear close to my face.

"Nothing," I said, disappointed that our special moment had to be interrupted this way.

Still holding the present, Jared cleared his throat. "Should I open it now?" he asked.

Suddenly I felt shy. "If you want to."

He ripped off the wrapping paper and stuffed it into his jeans pocket. Then, opening the clothbound book, he let out a low whistle. "Is this what I think it is?" He glanced at me. Then he read the title, *A Heart Full of Poetry: At Christmas*.

"Original poetry by Holly Meredith," I said, pleased by his response. I reached up and stuck the red ribbon on his head, giggling.

That's when he caught my arm and gave me a quick hug. "Thanks, Holly-Heart. You're too good to be true."

I was thankful for the semi-darkness. It hid the blood rushing to my cheeks.

"I'll read every word tonight when I get home," he promised.

My teeth were chattering.

"Hey, I'd better get you inside. It's freezing out here."

I was reluctant to return to the loud party atmosphere. Mostly because Jared hadn't surprised me yet with a gift. And time was running out.

Pastor Rob called everyone to the family room around the fireplace. Jared sat beside me on the floor during our devotional time.

Later, when the doorbell rang, I rushed to get it. Mom stood there, ready to drive me to the airport.

"Just a minute," I said, letting her in out of the cold. "I'll get my jacket."

"Take your time," she said, coming inside.

Dying for an explanation from Jared about the gift I was sure he was going to give me, I ran upstairs to get my jacket. Under the second pile of coats, I found my present from Joy. Putting it in my pocket, I headed for the stairs.

Halfway down, I noticed Paula and Jared standing in the corner of the living room, near the Christmas tree. I leaned on the railing. What were they doing? I kept watching, relieved that Mom was engaged in conversation with Pastor Rob.

My heart pounded as I observed the handsome twosome. Paula's dark, shoulder-length hair was pulled away from her face with an elegant hair clip. Her face glowed as she gazed at gorgeous Jared. He held something in his hands.

What was it? I stared at the small, square box wrapped in red paper and topped with a white lacy bow. Paula flashed her pearly whites as he handed the gift to her. My heart sank as he beamed down at her.

Choking back the tears, I yanked on my jacket and zipped it up. Quickly, I thanked Pastor Rob for a terrific party and, without saying good-bye to anyone, not even Andie, stumbled to the car in the cold and suddenly bleak December night.

9

When our plane landed in L.A., I was dying to get off. Being cooped up in an airplane with a chatterbox little sister is no fun when what you really want to do is replay in your head the events of a Christmas party gone wrong. Over and over.

I waited impatiently in the aisle for the man ahead of me. He was asking the flight attendant about the weather in Hong Kong. Just my luck! I wanted to sprint down the aisle and up the ramp, but it was impossible because zillions of people were getting off.

At last, the line began to move, and we inched our way to the baggage claim area. People stood around in short sleeves and shorts, welcoming loved ones home for Christmas.

California was the place to be by the looks of things. By comparison, Dressel Hills seemed dull with its sting of cold—wintry and otherwise.

Carrie and I lugged our ski jackets, gazing at the sea of faces. One face stood out among them all. Daddy!

He waved, and soon his arms were around us both. The spicy smell of his cologne brought back a world of memories, and I was grateful, at least, for one thing. Daddy had come for us—alone—without Saundra. I was in no mood to deal with her tonight.

"Your stepmom stayed home with Tyler because of the late hour, but I have a feeling they'll be waiting up for you," Daddy explained. "How was your flight?" he asked.

"A little bumpy," Carrie said, rubbing her eyes. It was only the second plane ride of her life. "But it went fast from Colorado to here." She continued to jabber on about the flight attendants, the snack, and the turbulence we experienced as we headed for the parking lot with the other holiday travelers.

Warm, humid air hit my face as I walked beside Daddy, holding Carrie's hand. Palm trees swayed under the lights as we found Daddy's car. Carrie slid into the leathery front seat while I climbed into the back.

Soon we were on the freeway, heading for Daddy's gorgeous beach house. An old Christmas tune came on the radio. "I'll be home for Christmas," the singer crooned.

Feelings of homesickness pricked my heart. Outside, the waves of the Pacific Ocean shimmered in the moonlight. I stared up at the moon. The same one was shining down on the mountains of Colorado. Thinking that made me feel more miserable than ever.

"It's the ocean!" Carrie said. She strained hard against her seat belt, staring out the window.

"Yes, but wait till you see the view from the house tomorrow morning," Daddy told her. He turned into a long, narrow drive. Palm trees lined the lane, casting moon shadows on the luxurious, wine-red car. "Saundra's making Chinese food for lunch tomorrow." He smiled. "How's that sound?"

"You canceled your luncheon?" I asked, hoping he wouldn't leave us alone with the wicked stepmother on our very first day here.

"It's been postponed until Monday," he replied.

I stole quick glances at him, wondering if we'd have time for a heart-to-heart talk. Then the house appeared out of nowhere.

Saundra stood outside on the porch, wearing a black-and-white polka dot dress and black heels. She greeted Carrie and me as we came up the walk. But she hugged and kissed Daddy as though he'd been gone for weeks. I tried to remember Mom doing that. It was easy, except when the new Mrs. Meredith spoke. "Welcome to our home, girls." Heavy perfume hung in the air.

"I'm thirsty," Carrie said, waiting for Daddy to bring the luggage up from the car.

"And I have to call Mom," I told Saundra, who held open the front door. It was decorated with an enormous Christmas wreath of dried red rosebuds and baby's breath.

A wiry boy with auburn hair and freckles zoomed past us, wearing his pajamas and bathrobe.

"Oh, there you are, Tyler," Saundra said. She turned to me. "Your stepbrother has been anxiously awaiting your arrival, Holly." She smiled broadly, her red lips glistening in the porch light. Then she introduced her son to Carrie.

Tyler grabbed Carrie's hand and pulled her into the house. I heard him say, "There's a surprise in your room that's way cool," and with that, they were gone.

I headed for the kitchen to call Mom. She would be waiting up, eager to know we had arrived safely. I glanced around at the enormous living room, brilliant with golden hues. A Christmas tree stood in the middle of an expansive wall of windows overlooking the ocean. It reminded me of another tree, a very simple one decorated with handmade ornaments—the tree at Pastor Rob's house. Then, like a roaring avalanche, the painful memories of the evening came sweeping back.

Swallowing the lump in my throat, I found the kitchen phone. No way did I want to sound sad when I talked to Mom. "We made it here just fine," I told her when she answered.

"Oh, good." She sounded relieved. "I'm praying you'll both have a wonderful time. And Holly?"

"Yes?"

"Merry Christmas."

"I miss you already," I said, aware of the lump creeping into my throat. Again.

"Me too, sweetie," she said. "I'll see you soon."

"I hope the time goes by fast," I said softly so no one would hear.

When I finished talking, Tyler appeared around the corner, ready to guide me to my room—down a long, winding Cinderella staircase, its railing adorned with evergreen and red velvet bows. Two large bedrooms with a sitting room between graced the lower level. Just as I had remembered.

Tyler took me into the bedroom where Carrie was. "Look!" He pointed to a telescope set on a tripod across the room. It was aimed toward the ocean.

"Fabulous," I whispered. "Is this yours?"

Tyler grinned. "It's my old one, but you two can use it for now." Carrie couldn't keep her hands off it. She adjusted the lens, peering through the peep hole again and again.

Then I turned to see Daddy standing in the doorway. He was piled up with luggage. Tyler dashed across the room to open the wide, oak closet doors.

"There's plenty of space to hang things," my father said, bringing Carrie's bags into the room. "Make yourselves at home, girls. We're glad you've come to spend the holidays with us."

Tyler seemed impatient, shifting from one foot to the other. It was obvious he had other plans in mind, which didn't include unpacking or organizing clothes.

I went into my own room to rescue my overnight case. My hair stuff and makeup were inside, as well as my locked diary. Saundra followed me to my room. "As soon as you're unpacked, Holly, we'll have a dish of ice cream." She stood in the doorway, watching my every move. "There are towels and linens in the bathroom closet if you want to freshen up." She motioned for Tyler to scoot.

"See you upstairs, Holly," he called.

"Okay," I said, wondering where this nine-year-old boy got all his confidence. I could've used some tonight at the party. The scene replayed in my mind. In my imagination, I actually marched up to Jared and gleefully ripped my present—*A Heart Full of Poetry*—out of his hands!

In the bathroom, I opened a corner cupboard filled with elegant linens. I chose a thick blue towel with birds embroidered on it and a washcloth to match. There were brightly colored tins filled with butterfly soaps—pink, soft blue, and mint green. I lifted a green one to my nose and breathed deeply. Mmm! Almost pepperminty—like Mom's tea back home in Dressel Hills. I wondered if she was sipping some right now.

Glancing at my watch, I saw that it was an hour later there. Nope, she was probably asleep by now. A twinge gripped me. I was already homesick for the angel of a mother I'd left behind. I longed for her gentle ways and listening ear. Of course, she couldn't remove my hurt, no one could. But her soft voice and loving eyes would let me know I could survive—even without Jared as my friend.

After a warm shower I was too tired to engage in small talk or eat ice cream upstairs with Daddy . . . and especially Saundra. So, clad in a bathrobe, I excused myself and headed back to the huge room that was to be mine for the next two weeks. The thought of acquiring this major privacy in my life eased the homesickness slightly.

Glancing at the strewn contents of my suitcase, I felt guilty about waiting till tomorrow to unpack. But I pushed the feeling aside and slipped between the silky sheets, reaching for my overnight case and a pen. Then I recorded the heartbreaking news of the day.

Friday, December 17. It's late and I'm so tired, but I have to write these words on paper so I won't explode. Jared Wilkins is absolutely despicable! More tomorrow . . .

I locked my diary with the key on the chain around my neck. Sliding the diary under the pillow next to mine, I reached for the massive emerald lamp poised on the oak table. In the darkness, I asked God to ease my pain and to please help me forget Jared Wilkins—ASAP!

10

During lunch the next day, I watched Daddy sprinkle soy sauce on his rice. Saundra sat to his left, passing seconds to him, only to have them refused. I wished she'd back off. How many times did he have to say he was dieting, anyhow?

I decided I wouldn't call her Saundra this visit. The way she pronounced it gave me the creeps! Besides, it wasn't polite to address her by her first name anyway. Calling her "stepmom" seemed somewhat cold even though it fit her austere personality. So I resolved to avoid calling her anything. At least for now.

Tyler sat across the table from me, rolling his eyes at everything his mother said. "Sit up straight, dear," she'd say. "Lean over your plate," or "Don't poke at your food." On and on.

Carrie seemed entertained by his antics, however. And Tyler milked it for all it was worth, acting out and being rewarded with giggles from Carrie. I could see the two of them were quite a pair. And Daddy and Saundra, er, Mrs. Meredith the Second, were also quite taken with each other. As for well matched, though, I didn't see how that could possibly be.

I couldn't help it; I thought of Jared. In many ways we were opposites. I was loyal and wouldn't even *think* of two-timing, but he. . . ? What he'd done was unforgivable, and after those special moments we'd spent together on the deck . . . *"I'll read every word when I get home,"* Jared had said about my book of poetry. I wanted to wring his neck—Paula's, too! It was all her fault, stepping in on my territory. Again.

Andie's advice rang in my ears. *Ignore Paula.*

Right! How could I when it was obvious that Jared couldn't?

Daddy reached for Saundra's hand and squeezed it. They were quite a couple. Where did that leave me? Furiously, I snapped open a fortune cookie. The thin strip of paper stuck out, but I crumpled it without reading it and stuffed it into my shorts pocket despite Saundra's disapproving look.

Tyler excused himself, and he and Carrie ran off to play. Daddy kissed Saundra and left the table, too. Saundra sat across from me, her reddish hair swept up away from her face. Wisps of hair dangled in ringlets near her ears.

Uncomfortable with the silence, I attempted to clear the table, but she interfered immediately, declaring that this was my vacation and I was not to lift a finger to help in any way.

Okay, I thought. *I can handle that.* I wandered off to find Daddy—the perfect excuse to avoid direct conversation with her.

Daddy's study was lined with wall-to-wall books, shelved in rich, glowing cherrywood. Not surprising—everything in this house was polished to a high gleam. I stared in amazement at his collection of books, ignoring the thought that some of them probably belonged to Saundra.

I tiptoed behind Daddy's chair and peeked over the back. He was reading a book of poetry. He chuckled. "Mice are quieter than you," he said, motioning for me to sit on his hassock. "What's on your mind?"

"You are," I said courageously, curious about the poetry he was reading.

He held it up, surveying the title. "It's free verse," he said. "What's your taste in poetry?"

"Rhyming's my favorite."

"That figures," he said, with a faint smile. "Your mother always preferred it over a loose rhyme pattern, too." He mentioned her so effortlessly, I wondered if he thought of Mom often.

"You remember?" I asked, feeling uncomfortable with his easygoing approach.

He nodded, touching my head as I knelt beside his chair. "There are many happy memories." His crisp, articulate voice turned suddenly soft and intimate.

Deep and dark, The Question stirred within me. *Now!* it urged me. *Ask now!*

My lips formed The Question, but the words remained locked up. Dense pain concealed it, forcing it down . . . deep into the most secret places of my being.

"I've missed so much of your life, Holly," Daddy was saying. Unexpectedly, he wrapped his arms around me. I hugged him back, feeling some of the pain of those lost years.

And then, he was reading a winter sonnet, the sound of his voice soothing me, even though the poem reminded me of cold, snowy Colorado. I didn't mind. Having Daddy all to myself like this was sweet.

Just then, Saundra broke the spell by carrying in a tray of sodas for three. She sat across the room, silently sipping hers. I cringed. The special moment had ended for me with Saundra's intrusion. I felt cheated . . . and hurt.

That night in my journal I had a few choice words to say about my wicked stepmother.

♥　♥　♥

I awakened to knocks at my door the next morning.

"Yes?" I answered sleepily.

"I fixed breakfast for you," Tyler announced through the door. "May I come in?"

Sitting up, I reached for one of the many pillows piled up on my enormous bed. I pulled the covers up to my chest and called, "Okay."

Slowly, Tyler emerged, straining to balance a breakfast tray of scrambled eggs and jelly toast, a tiny glass of orange juice, and a tall glass of milk.

"You did all this?"

He looked embarrassed, but only for a second. "I'm way good at making breakfast."

"Thanks, Tyler," I said, spreading out the white linen napkin. "Does your mom know you used her cloth napkin?"

"Oh yes," he said, his golden-brown eyes smiling. "She insisted on it."

I poked a piece of scrambled egg and remembered I'd forgotten to pray. I put my fork down.

"It's safe to eat. Honest," he exclaimed.

"I believe you," I replied. "But I always pray before I eat."

"Always?" he asked, raising his eyebrows.

I nodded. "Wanna join me?"

"I don't know how," he said.

"It's not hard," I explained. "It's like talking to your best friend."

"I heard a man pray on the radio once. He had lots of thees and thous in his prayer."

"God doesn't care if our words are perfect or not. He wants our hearts," I said, delighted to share my faith with Tyler again.

"Will you pray out loud so I can listen?" he asked sheepishly.

I nodded. "Dear Lord," I began, "this breakfast looks fabulous. Thanks for blessing it and thanks for Tyler, who put it all together as a special surprise for me. In Jesus' name, Amen."

"Wow, that's way easy," Tyler said.

I smiled. "Wanna try tonight at supper?"

"Nah," he said, stepping back. "My mom would have a cow."

"How come?"

"She's not much into God and stuff like that," he said, turning to leave.

"Where are you going now?" I asked.

"Carrie's next," he said, grinning at me over his shoulder. I picked up my fork and sampled the eggs. Suddenly Tyler was back. "Here, I forgot to give you this," he said, handing me a note.

It was from Daddy. The note said he had an unexpected appointment, and Saundra was out doing last-minute Christmas shopping. *Do you mind watching Tyler and Carrie for a few hours while we're gone?* It was signed, *Love, Daddy.*

Tyler stood in the doorway. "Enjoy your breakfast while I plan our day." A sudden mischievous look spread across his freckled face. "The house is empty, and it's almost Christmas!"

The gleam in his eyes gave away his secret. The little sneak!

"Carrie! Wake up!" he called to her. "I'm serving you breakfast in bed." His voice trailed off, but I heard something about raiding the closets and looking under the beds for presents.

Yikes! I had my work cut out for me babysitting these two. I gobbled down the rest of my breakfast and, finding my robe, finished unpacking. Before I made the bed, I pulled my diary out of hiding, making sure it was still locked. No one needed to know about my troubles back in Dressel Hills.

I opened the drapes and gazed out at the ocean. Sea gulls drifted lazily in the warmth of the sun. Soaking up the breathtaking view, I talked to God. It was Sunday morning in Daddy's house. Back home, we'd all be in church by now. I felt a twinge of sadness for the free and easy lifestyle Daddy was accustomed to. And Tyler . . . How could a kid make it growing up without God in his life? I blamed Saundra for her disinterest in spiritual things. I poured out my thoughts and feelings. Before long, I was soothed as I watched the waves crash in with the tide.

My gaze found a boy running along the beach, a black Labrador at his side. Every so often, the boy would stop, rub the Lab's back, and talk to her. There was no question about their relationship—they were good pals.

I leaned on the arm of the overstuffed chair for a longer look. Printed on the boy's blue sweat shirt was the number thirty-four. Tan with sun-bleached blond hair, he was about Stan's age, I guessed. I watched till he was a speck in the distance.

Reluctantly, I turned away from the window to make my bed and then hurried off to check on Tyler and Carrie. But my thoughts curiously centered on Number Thirty-four.

11

"Disappear!" Carrie shouted as I entered her bedroom. "This is *my* room!"

"Give me a break," I said, bending down to pick up pajamas, underwear, you-name-it.

"Sure, I'll give you a break," she snapped. "Tyler and I are going outside to the hot tub, how's that?" With a flick of her long hair, my sister flounced off to the bathroom, swimsuit in hand.

"Fine," I muttered, sitting on the edge of her unmade bed.

When she finally emerged, Carrie's hair flopped around in a ponytail high on her head, and a towel hung over her bare shoulders.

"Nice suit," I said.

"Saundra bought it for me." She pushed a pile of rumpled clothes off the chair. Then she dug into a department store bag and pulled out a hot-pink two-piece bathing suit and threw it at me.

"Where'd you get this?" I asked, holding it up.

"It's for you, from your wicked stepmother!"

Our eyes caught for a second, then Carrie glanced away, her face filled with guilt.

"Why, you little . . ." I grabbed her arm, ready to accuse her of reading my diary. But wait . . . it was locked this morning when I checked—and I was wearing the key! I glared at her. "How'd you do it?"

Carrie knew exactly what I meant. "Easy," she taunted, pulling away from me.

Tyler stood in the doorway, wearing his swimming trunks. "What's going on?" he asked.

Carrie shouted, "This is what happens when you're not the only child. Be thankful."

I wanted to shake her. "Stop avoiding the subject and stay away from my diary."

Carrie faced Tyler, still ignoring me. I reached out to grab her, but she spun away and ran upstairs as I followed her into the hallway.

Tyler shrugged his shoulders. "You two fight like this at home?" he asked. Then he turned and ran upstairs, yelling for Carrie. I stormed off to my room and sat near the window, creating a plan to catch my sister red-handed. Tonight!

♥ ♥ ♥

After a long morning of swimming and supervising Tyler and Carrie, I should've been wiped out by the end of this day. But I wasn't the least bit tired at ten-thirty when I turned off the light.

Pulling up the sheet, I waited. I was almost sure what Carrie was doing. While I slept, she would unlock my diary with the key around my neck. I didn't know exactly how, without waking me, but I was known to be a heavy sleeper. So . . . even if it meant staying up all night, I was determined to catch her!

After what seemed like hours, I glanced at the clock on my lamp table. Only eleven. Surely Carrie would come sneaking in any minute.

In the darkness, I crept to the window and watched moonbeams promenade across the ocean. And then I saw something moving along the beach. Inching closer to the window, I spied a large animal running on the beach beside a jogger. I strained to see. Then I remembered the telescope.

Hurrying to Carrie's room, I tiptoed to the long, black tube poised on a tripod. Glancing across the room, I checked out my sleeping sister. Then, positioning the lens, I brought it into focus.

Number Thirty-four! His sleek black Labrador ran at his side. I sharpened the focus, pulling the tall, blond boy into closer range. I could see him clearly now, his dark green sweats and his bare feet.

Carrie stirred in her sleep. I squatted down, holding my breath. When I was certain she was asleep again, I left quickly.

Instead of counting sheep after I slipped between the sheets, I counted the days Jared and I had been together before the Christmas party. I could still hear his voice whispering my nickname. *Holly-Heart* . . .

Tears trickled over my cheeks and landed in my ears as I stared up at the ceiling. A stream of precious words tumbled back into my consciousness. *I miss you. Can't wait to see you at church. One less hour till I see you. You're too good to be true, Holly-Heart.*

I turned over and pressed my face into the pillow, closing my eyes and squeezing the tears out. The old days and my new Jared were gone, thanks to Paula Miller.

♥   ♥   ♥

The next morning I woke with a start.

Yikes—I'd fallen asleep! I slid my hand under the pillow next to me and felt for my diary and the lock. Both were secure. So was the key on the chain around my neck.

Glancing at the clock, I discovered it was only six forty-five. But I was too wide awake to go back to sleep. I wandered over to the windows and sat on the chair in the corner. Sea gulls screeched as they did their morning exercises over the ocean waves.

Exercise. Just what I needed. I pulled on some shorts and a T-shirt and headed outside for a walk on the beach.

The salty sea breeze energized me. I ran hard, barefooted on the wet sand, as the breakers came in with the tide. Eventually I slowed to a walk, closing my eyes, facing the first rays of the sun. Here it was, four days till Christmas, and it felt like summer. But something was missing, and it wasn't just the snow. It was much more than that. Mom was back home, and I missed her. Andie wasn't around for me to cry on her shoulder. And Jared . . . What was to become of us? Thinking that thought made me teary eyed again. I was truly homesick.

I decided to take things into my own hands. There would be Christmas cheer right here on this beach, even if I had to make a snowman out of sand. I stooped down and began pushing damp sand into a large ball. Soon I had a jolly, round base, and I stepped back for a quick look.

An hour or so later, someone called to me. "Holly!"

I turned to see Carrie and Tyler running toward my sand creation at full speed. Anger churned inside me when I saw Carrie, her long golden locks flying in the ocean's breeze. It still bugged me, not being able to keep a nosy little sister out of my very private diary.

"Wow, that's huge!" Tyler exclaimed when he saw the round sand ball. "What're you making?"

"I know!" Carrie shrieked with delight. "It's gonna be a sandy snowman."

"Way cool," Tyler said. "Can we help?"

"Run to the house and get something to carry water in," I told him, and off he went.

Now that Carrie and I were alone, I was dying to continue the tongue-lashing she rightfully deserved. Eyeing me nervously she said, "You won't tell Mommy, will you?"

"Of course I'll tell, and that's not the only thing I'll do," I said, thinking about how fabulous it would be to see the look on her face tonight when I reached out from under the covers and scared the living daylights out of her.

"Tell me!" she demanded.

"No way." I brushed the sand off my knees.

Glancing up, I saw Tyler racing toward us, waving something.

"This just came," he said, shoving a white envelope marked "Two-Day Priority Mail" into my sandy hand.

"Thanks." I searched for a spot of dry sand to sit on.

"We're having brunch in ten minutes," Tyler said. "My mother said so." He made a face, laughing.

"I'm not hungry," I said, opening the letter.

"I am!" Carrie pulled off her sandals and ran, splashing into the ocean with Tyler. "Tell us when ten minutes are up," she called back to me.

"Whatever," I muttered, anxious to read my best friend's letter.

> *Hey, Heartless:*
> *I would've sent this overnight express mail, but do you know how expensive that is? Anyway, this was the best I could afford, and I just had to write because something weird's happening. My best friend (that's you, in case you forgot) leaves for her fancy-tancy Christmas in California without saying good-bye! Where's your heart, Holly? I mean, it's bad enough having to suffer through the holidays without someone to CONFIDE in, if you know what I mean?*
> *And for starters, Stan likes me. Can you believe it, your cousin likes ME, after all that flirting*

to get his attention? Well, it worked, and Holly, is
he ever nice! He's so-o-o-o fine! If only you were
here, I could tell you everything . . .

Now for the big, bad stuff. You are in deep
water with Jared. He couldn't believe you left without telling him good-bye. Anyway, neither of us
knew what happened to you. He was totally
shocked that you would leave like that. I looked for
you after the devotional, and poof, you were gone!
That's NOT the way to treat your best friend, not
to mention a guy like Jared—especially when you
wrote those poems for him. (Yep, he let me read
one of them.) And, hey, you're good. Jared thinks
so, too. He misses you, Holly—a lot!

Would ya please write soon? Hugs for Christmas!

Love,
Andie

I refolded the letter and pushed it into the
envelope. Andie didn't know what she was talking about. Jared had everyone fooled, even my
best friend. If only she'd seen Jared standing in
the corner with Paula, giving her that little gift
all wrapped up so sweet. Pathetic Paula made me
sick!

I glanced at my watch. "Ten minutes are up," I called to Carrie and Tyler, who ran like hungry bandits to the house.

Carrie called back to me. "Aren't you coming?"

I shook my head as I stuffed Andie's letter into my pocket. I needed more time to sit here in the sun. Staring out at the horizon, I contemplated life and love and Jared Wilkins.

And then I heard Saundra's proper-sounding voice. I should've expected she'd insist I come inside for something to eat. Her vocal cords strained a bit as she called again, "Holly, dear, time for brunch!"

Here was another female who made me sick. Sick Saundra. Hmm, wasn't very nice, but oh well—it fit her just fine.

"No, thanks," I shouted. She shook her head as she went inside.

♥   ♥   ♥

By the time Carrie and Tyler returned, I was ready to finish making Sandy, my snowman substitute. Tyler lugged a grocery bag filled with containers of different sizes.

"Perfect," I said, reaching for a plastic pitcher and heading for the ocean. It was fun smoothing and rounding out the three parts of Sandy: his base, stomach, and head. When it was time for his eyes, nose, and mouth, I let Tyler and Carrie in on the decision making.

"What about seashell ears?" Carrie suggested.

"Cool," Tyler said, grinning.

I agreed.

"How about garland for his neck?" Tyler said. "I bet my mom has some left over."

"Good idea," Carrie said.

"Don't forget the holly," a strange voice came from behind me.

We turned to see a tall, blond boy holding out a stiff, shiny leaf with a cluster of bright red berries on it. His black Labrador stood panting at his side. It was Number Thirty-four—and for a second, I thought he was saying my name.

"Hey, thanks." Tyler snatched the fake holly leaf out of the jogger's hand. He acted like he knew him! Then Tyler said, "Where should we put it?"

"Stick it in his ear," shouted Carrie before the tall stranger could answer.

In a flash, Tyler reached up and pushed the holly stem into the hardened sand above one of the seashell ears. "Fantastic," he yelled.

"All he needs now is a hat," Number Thirty-four said with a soft chuckle. Tyler poked him in the ribs and ran down the beach toward the house.

Curious, I leaned down to pet the black Labrador. "Nice dog," I said, feeling a bit shy.

Carrie piped up. "What's her name?"

Number Thirty-four, dressed in a T-shirt and cargo shorts, responded with a grin. "Sunshine. She's my jogging partner." He leaned down to rub the Lab's side. "Aren't you, girl?" The beautiful dog nuzzled close.

"Why'd you name her that?" I asked, wishing Carrie had followed Tyler into the house.

"Lots of people ask that." He gave a light-hearted chuckle. "I tell them you can't be fooled by her color. Underneath this black coat, there's a heart of gold."

I nodded, careful not to seem too curious. "You live around here?"

"About three miles down the beach," he said, pointing in the direction. Then he bent down and picked up a clump of wet sand, shaping it with his long fingers, tan like the rest of his body. The Lab sat at attention nearby. "You're here for the holidays, right?"

"We're from Colorado," Carrie announced as she worked on our snowman substitute.

He nodded, helping Carrie smooth out a bumpy patch of sand. "How's that?"

"What about this?" she asked, pointing to a drooping seashell ear.

Number Thirty-four reached up to secure it, then, on second thought, stopped and leaned over to hoist Carrie onto his shoulders. "You fix it."

Carrie giggled, reaching for the ear.

"Tyler told me he was getting company for Christmas. How do you like it here so far?" the blond boy asked, balancing Carrie.

I twisted the ends of my hair. "California's nice. Uh . . . and I was here last summer for almost a month, but now, the winter, well, it doesn't seem like Christmas without snow." I felt tongue-tied. Why couldn't I talk to this guy?

A broad grin swept across his face. "Maybe you'll change your mind after two weeks."

Two weeks? What else did he know about us?

He turned his attention back to "Sandy." Slowly, an elf-like shoe began to take shape under his hands. Number 34 was careful to create the next shoe slightly different from the first. Soon, two clever feet stuck out of Sandy's base.

"Looks perfect," I said, still wondering why he was hanging around. But more than that, I wondered why my heart seemed to speed up when his hazel eyes caught mine.

In a minute, Tyler was back with a forest green hat. It looked like a lady's felt hat, complete with a cream-colored silk flower.

"That looks silly," Carrie said.

"It's the only one I could find," Tyler responded.

"Too risky," I whispered to myself before telling Tyler not to use it on Sandy. I had enough problems coping with my stepmom without being responsible for destroying her expensive wardrobe.

"Guess you're right," Tyler said, shaking the hat a bit too enthusiastically. "Oh, by the way, Holly, my mom wants to take you Christmas shopping this afternoon."

"How do you know?" I felt funny discussing the plans of the day while Number Thirty-four eavesdropped.

"Because she just said so," Tyler answered, grabbing the tan boy's arm and playfully swatting at him. "And guess who's baby-sitting!"

"Fine with me," Number Thirty-four said. "And are we still on for tomorrow?"

"Oh yeah, I almost forgot," Tyler admitted. "Do you two wanna go bodysurfing with Sean and me?"

Sean? *The hottie has a name*, I thought, almost forgetting the question Tyler had just posed.

"I'm going whether Holly does or not," Carrie announced. She ran in and out of the tide, splashing against the beach.

Sean tapped his knee, and Sunshine promptly moved to his side. "Well, that's *three* of us." Sean turned to me, waiting, it seemed, for my answer.

"Sounds like fun." My heart skipped a beat, the way it used to when Jared winked at me. It was very strange, my response to Sean.

"Holly, dear." It was Saundra calling from the beach house balcony. She waved her arms, trying to attract my attention.

"Coming!" I called. *No sense keeping the dragon lady waiting.*

"Nice meeting you, Holly," Sean said, flinging Tyler over his shoulder, then stopping to extend his hand to me.

I accepted his handshake like an adult. "Same here," I answered.

"Wait," Tyler shouted. "Don't forget the hat." He leaped out of Sean's grasp, picked up his mother's felt hat, and tossed it to me. A slight breeze caught it, and up it flew like a Frisbee.

I reached for it and missed. "Oh, fabulous," I muttered, picking it up and gently shaking it off. Now the hat thing was on *me*, and unfortunately it wasn't the best topic for opening remarks. Not Saundra's hat—no consignment shop special, for sure—dusty with beach sand.

Brushing away thoughts of the wicked stepmother, I focused on Sean and the momentary touch of his hand on mine.

The memory lingered, warm as a glove, as I headed toward the beach house.

13

Promptly placing Saundra's hat on the deck chaise lounge, I scurried into the house.

Saundra did her scrutiny number on me first off. "I'll be happy to wait for you to shower and change into something more appropriate," was the first thing out of her mouth. "And you haven't had a thing to eat," was next. "You must be starving." She punctuated her words with a deep sigh.

I hurried downstairs to the shower. Good thing she hadn't seen the hat.

After my shower, I discovered a tray of fruit and a sandwich sliced into mini-sections on the dresser in my room. *Should've known*, I thought, reaching for some grapes.

On the bed, I spied the hot-pink two-piece outfit where I'd left it. "This is going back from whence it came," I protested out loud, remembering the surfing date, er, plans Tyler, Carrie, and I had made with Sean. No way would I be caught dead in this scant little number in front of a boy.

I slipped into a gray cotton skirt and a blue top. Surely *this* was appropriate enough for Christmas shopping with Saundra. After brushing my hair and applying some fresh makeup, I hid the letter from Andie under the bed pillow, next to my diary. Then, snatching up the two-piece bathing suit, I hurried upstairs.

Saundra was waiting on the deck in a smart navy-and-white dress. Red shoes and purse completed her outfit. I swallowed hard, hoping she wouldn't comment on the hat lying on the chaise. At least now it was sand-free.

"We'll head for the mall first," she announced, getting up from a white wicker patio chair. The wicker reminded me of my mother's house—the bathroom cupboard where I'd hidden my diary key and fallen into the toilet.

"What's that in your hand, dear?" She interrupted my thoughts, eyeing the almost-bikini I carried.

"Oh, this." I acknowledged Saundra's inquisitive look. I took a deep breath. "It's just not me," I told her flat out. "But I *will* be needing one for tomorrow, so if you don't mind, I'd like to exchange it for something a little more . . ."

"Absolutely," she said, snatching up the green felt hat as we headed inside. "You may choose whatever you like, dear."

Dear this, *dear* that. I cringed. Why did everything have to end with terms of endearment?

Inside, she hung the hat in the closet near the front door without saying a word. Then we headed for the garage. She unlocked the car doors with the touch of a button on her key ring. I settled into the jazzy white sports car, amazed at the super plush interior. The dashboard was almost as bright as her red shoes and purse. But I wasn't surprised. Everything about Saundra was super flashy and expensive.

♥　♥　♥

At the mall, Saundra waited outside the dressing room (thank goodness) while I tried on another swimsuit. A rainbow of colors—blues, pinks, and lavender—it looked fabulous on me. Much better than the two-piece Saundra had chosen. At least this one concealed my skinny ribs and hip bones. But it did show something. I turned sideways in the floor-length mirror to admire my developing physique. Perfect! Well . . . getting there.

The swimsuit dilemma solved, I felt less reluctant about spending the entire afternoon shopping with Daddy's wife. Of course, I didn't let on to her.

Next we browsed in a candle boutique, where Saundra purchased a dozen gold candles, all different lengths. "Won't these look lovely on the mantel on Christmas Eve?" she commented, half to me, half to the air.

I nodded as she strolled regally to the counter. She exchanged small talk with the clerk, and I continued to survey her from afar. How could Daddy have picked her for his wife? She was so . . . fakey. I heard her say to the clerk, "Merry Christmas, hon. Keep the change."

Well, there was one thing Saundra had going for her. She was benevolent. That was okay, I guess, if she wasn't your stepmom. A faint recognition stirred within me. Yep, that was a big part of why I didn't like her. She wasn't daddy's *first* wife. She wasn't Mom—not even close.

"Do we have time for a quick stop at the card shop?" she asked, as if she actually cared about what I wanted to do.

It amused me, but I kept the smile hidden inside and the icy stare frozen to my face. "Whatever," I stated flatly. My sullen attitude didn't seem to faze her, however, and we marched to the nearest Hallmark shop. Inside, she went her way and I went mine. In the Christmas card section I pulled out a gorgeous card with zillions of hearts decorating it. "First Christmas together" was written in fancy lettering across the top.

Staring at the couple painted on the card, I drew in a faltering breath. It was obvious the twosome were in love by the way they stood, hand in hand, gazing at each other.

The card stirred up the old homesickness in me. Suddenly I deeply missed Dressel Hills. But more than that, I longed for my friendship with Jared. I wanted things the way they were—*before* Paula!

Oh, Jared, why did you have to go and spoil everything? my heart cried. *How could you say all those things? Those wonderful things . . .*

My eyes filled with tears. Out of control, they brimmed over the edge, rolling down my cheeks.

"Get over it, girl," I muttered, frantically searching for the cards that matched the one in my hand. Through the tears, things were a blur. I grabbed for a tissue, in my pocket, in my purse. Anywhere. "Get a grip," I whispered angrily, pushing the card in anywhere it fit.

Then I snatched a red envelope from another stack and shoved it in front of the First

Christmas Together card, hiding it from view.

No way can I let Saundra see me like this, I thought, determined to rid myself of any trace of emotion. I pulled out a ratty tissue from my pocket and darted behind the counter display of jewelry boxes. One of them had a mirror inside its lid, and I stooped down to dry my eyes, dabbing at my cheeks.

"May I help you?" a clerk asked, appearing out of nowhere.

Speechless, I shook my head. Evidently she mistook my silence for extraordinary interest and began winding the music box of one of the most exquisite jewelry cases on display.

The song, "Someday My Prince Will Come," began to spill into the air. Into my heart. Desperately, I wanted to run from the store. Instead, my eye makeup ran as more tears streamed down my cheeks. I was sobbing in the middle of a card shop in Southern California, five days before Christmas. It was nuts, but I couldn't help it.

Just then Saundra spotted me, and when she saw my tears, her face fell. At first I thought she was embarrassed. But as she approached, I saw something else.

"Holly, dear," she whispered, "let's go somewhere quiet." And before I could respond, she ushered me, unnoticed, out of the store.

By the time we arrived in front of a doughnut

shop, my tears had subsided. I stuffed the frayed tissue into my pocket and, dying of humiliation, wracked my brain. What was wrong with me? Crying in public?

"Would you like something to eat, or would you rather I take you home?" Saundra asked gently.

It was strange. I wasn't ready for the shopping spree to end. "I'll be okay," I said.

"Are you sure?"

"Yes, thanks," I said, meaning it.

Saundra ordered two sodas and a cream-filled doughnut for me. I was amazed at her memory. Last summer during my visit, I'd chosen cream-filled doughnuts to surprise Daddy one morning at breakfast. Five months ago.

"Would you care for anything else, dear?" she asked, minus the inquisition I was sure would follow my tearful outburst. She handed me several clean tissues.

"This is fine, thanks," I replied, then blew my nose. While I sipped my pop, Saundra pulled a pad of paper from her purse. I could see three different lists printed neatly on one page. "I make lists all the time," I remarked, almost without thinking.

She tapped on the second list, smiling briefly. "This is the only way I've found I can ever manage things." She copied one of the lists onto another page and handed it to me. "Here are some ideas for your father's Christmas gift, in case you need some hints." She pulled out her wallet and handed over a wad of twenty-dollar bills. "I thought you'd want to buy something special for him, for you and Carrie to present to him at Christmas. If you'd like, we could meet back here in, say, an hour or so."

I nodded, still in semi-shock at so much money thrust into my hand. "I have my own money from home," I said. "I won't need this much."

"Don't worry about it, dear. If there's any left, feel free to spend it however you please," she said. "Who knows, maybe you'll see something you can't live without." She looked at her watch. "I have twenty-till-two. Shall we synchronize our time?"

"Good idea," I said, moving the minute hand on my watch to match hers.

"I'll see you here in about an hour," she promised, waving her hand, adorned with bright red, fake fingernails.

"Okay," I called, feeling lighter, brighter. After all, it was almost Christmas. Jesus' birthday. If only I could focus on the true meaning of this razzle-dazzle time of year, I'd be fine. With or without Jared Wilkins.

Saundra's list gave me zillions of ideas for Daddy, but there was one item missing from the list. Saundra had forgotten about his poetry obsession. I headed for the Christian bookstore with the *perfect* gift in mind. With a little help from the store clerk, I found a beautiful hardback version of the Psalms. It would be a sneaky way of introducing him to the Bible and its lyrical Psalms. Free verse—just the way he liked it.

Next I found a present for Tyler—a book on creation, lavishly illustrated and written in terms a kid could understand. Tyler had said his mom would "have a cow" about God and religious stuff, but today I had the urge to risk it. I hoped I was doing the right thing.

Tons of stocking stuffers took up most of the rest of Saundra's money. But there was still something I had to buy. Heading back to the card shop, I bypassed the card section and found a leather-covered organizer, the perfect gift for a list-making stepmom. A warm feeling came over me as I paid for the gift. With my own money.

♥   ♥   ♥

The next day, Tyler, Carrie, and I ate a hearty breakfast of waffles and scrambled eggs.

"You'll have to wait thirty minutes before swimming," Saundra said, clearing off the dining room table.

Tyler protested, as usual. "But, Mom," he whined, "we're not gonna be swimming, we're using the body boards." This time it was Saundra who rolled her eyes.

Carrie pulled Tyler out of the kitchen. "C'mon, you can't play till you make your bed," she informed him.

I grinned at that. What did Carrie know about making beds and keeping a clean bedroom? I snickered as I began helping with the dishes. Surprisingly, Saundra didn't launch a protest this time. We worked in silence for a while. Then I glanced at her. "Thanks for being so understanding yesterday at the mall," I said, putting away the maple syrup.

She gathered up the linen napkins, soiled with sticky syrup and butter. "It's one of those emotional things that happen from time to time," she said.

She probably had no idea what I was really thanking her for, but I had made an attempt at least. "Christmas is a rotten time to have boy problems." I paused, feeling awkward about opening up too much of myself.

"I can certainly relate to that," Saundra admitted, pulling a chair out and sitting at the table with a cup of coffee. "My former husband decided to leave a few weeks before Christmas. Tyler was only two, so he didn't understand. Neither did I." She leaned her arm against the table.

I stopped loading the dishes and looked at her. Really looked at her. This woman—my wicked stepmom, or so I called her—had experienced some of the same feelings my own mother had years before, when Daddy left us. I didn't care to know the details of how she and Daddy met or anything like that. Not now. But one thing was certain, she seemed to understand how I'd felt in the card shop yesterday.

Without thinking, I touched her shoulder. "It must've been hard, going through that Christmas," I said, a wave of sadness sweeping over me.

Saundra reached up and stroked my hand. "All of that is in the past now," she said with a smile. "Your father and I are very happy together."

Just then Carrie came upstairs, yelling something about Tyler heading for the beach without her. "He said by the time he gets down there, it'll be exactly thirty minutes since he swallowed his last bite."

"That's fine, dear," Saundra said, pushing a stray hair into a gold clip at the back of her neck.

I excused myself, assuming our chat was over. Back downstairs, I hurried to Carrie's room and peeked into the telescope. Focusing the lens, I could see Tyler hauling the body boards toward the beach. Soon Carrie came running down the sandy slope toward him.

Slowly, I moved the telescope, scanning the area near the kids. But it wasn't the kids I was spying on. Where was Sean? I couldn't wait to see him. That wonderful laugh, and the way he treated Carrie and Tyler . . . I was sure he'd make a fabulous father someday, when he was all grown up.

And then, there he was. In full view of this magnificent telescope. Tall, tan—gorgeous. He raced over to the kids, his black Lab running beside him. When he got to Carrie, he picked her up and swung her around. *Just like Uncle Jack,* I thought.

Then I watched as Sean pointed to the

house. My heart leaped up. Had Sean asked about *me*?

Hurrying to my room, I got ready for a day of fun on the beach. Before leaving, I pulled back the bedspread and slid my hand under the pillow. Grabbing my diary, I slipped the chain off my neck and unlocked the secrets of my life. As I flipped through the pages, locating today's date, I noticed sticky fingerprints on several pages. Maple syrup! We'd had waffles this morning. The truth clobbered me. Carrie had read my diary again. But how?

I scrutinized the private passages she surely must have seen, the telltale signs marking the truth. I burned with rage. "That sneaky little brat," I whispered.

At this very moment, my sister had full knowledge of my secret desire—to own Mom's heart locket, the one Daddy had given her the day I was born.

In the bathroom, I wiped the sticky smudges off the pages as my anger mixed with mounting fear. My dearest wish must be treated with reverence! Unfortunately, I knew Carrie couldn't be trusted.

Grabbing a dainty hand towel, I patted the wet spots around the edges of my diary. Worry for other matters clouded my thinking. Carrie had, no doubt, read my choice words about Jared, as well, not to mention the detailed account of the Christmas party last Friday night. And, worse than any of it, she'd read about my growing interest in Sean.

I glanced out the window. Part of me longed to go out and ride the waves. Yet I was afraid if I went outside now, I'd yell and scream and call Carrie names. Not a nice thing for a big sister to do, especially in front of a cute guy who had an obvious soft spot in his heart for kids.

I knelt beside my bed and talked to God about everything. Finally I could pray without pounding my fist against the bed. I wanted the Lord to show me how Carrie was sneaking into my private writings. "After all," I prayed, "you do know *all* things."

I stopped for a moment, contemplating the problems of the day. "And, Lord, I need your help about something else. It's Saundra. Help me forgive her for marrying Daddy and taking him away from us." It was a difficult prayer, one I'd been avoiding.

♥   ♥   ♥

The sun was high in the sky by the time I sauntered outside and down the well-worn path.

A gentle breeze stirred the tall grass on either side of the slope.

"Holly!" called Tyler, bobbing in the ocean. "Surf's up!"

I spied Sean steadying Carrie's board as she hopped on. Together they rode a medium-sized wave accompanied by my sister's squeals of glee.

I could see this was going to be a great day. Then I remembered Carrie's dreadful deed. My heart pounded as she came up to me.

"Wanna ride next?" she asked innocently.

I forced a smile, mainly because Sean was only a few feet away.

"Hey, Holly," Sean said, a dazzling smile dancing across his face.

"Looks like fun," I managed to say.

Sean came around and walked beside me. "Let's race."

I didn't have the nerve to tell him this was my first time surfing.

Carrie piped up, though. "My sister's never done this before. C'mon, Holly," she bossed, "I'll show you what to do."

Sean stepped in front of her, grabbing both her arms. "Whoa there, young lady," he said with great charm. "You'd better let me do the honors."

I felt my face grow warm. Maybe he wouldn't notice. Maybe he'd think I was sunburned.

Anyway, Carrie continued to interfere playfully.

"Guess I'll just have to dunk you," he said, flipping Carrie over his shoulder and marching into the water.

"No, no! Put me down!" Her shouts mingled with laughter.

It was perfect. Carrie had it coming, and I followed to make sure she got a thorough drenching.

Jumping in and out of the shallow waves, I worked my way out to Sean. When it came time for the actual dunking, he was careful. He even held Carrie's nose shut. Then down he took her, pulling her quickly out. Carrie loved it—the attention, that is. And I enjoyed watching Sean and his playful yet gentle way with my little sister.

Swimming back toward shore, Sean leaped out of the water and grabbed a surfboard near the beach towel where Sunshine dozed. "Watch this," he called to us.

Curiously I watched as he whistled to Sunshine, long and low. The Lab's eyes popped open. Then Sean sprinted through the foam at the water's edge, the board under his arm as he threw himself into a wave.

The sleek, black dog leaped off the towel and into the ocean, swimming toward the calmer water farther out.

Treading water, I watched as Sean pushed the board under Sunshine. Standing up, the dog rode the board—rising and falling with the moving water. Then, up . . . up she went with the swell and roar of the wave, riding the crest as it pounded the surf.

Crash! The wave fizzled to foam and the ride was over.

"Fabulous!" I said. "Did you teach her that?"

Sean nodded, obviously pleased with Sunshine's performance. Then he dove under water, swimming to retrieve the surfboard. "Who's next?" he asked, grinning.

"I'll try it!" Carrie shouted.

"How about some more practice with the body board?" he suggested.

Sean was cautious, and I liked that. Reckless guys had never impressed me.

I floated lazily on my back as the warm California sun shone down. What a perfect way to spend the holidays. I'd gone California crazy just like Uncle Jack had warned. . . .

♥   ♥   ♥

The day sped by so quickly, and I was sad to see it end.

Carrie and Tyler had actually left me alone with Sean occasionally. By suppertime, I was reluctant to say good-bye to my new friend.

"I have an idea," he said as I wrapped myself in a towel. "Meet me here at dusk on Christmas Eve. We'll walk along the beach for a while." He never winked or flirted or anything, but in his face there was eagerness. It excited me and made me nervous at the same time.

"Sounds good, but . . ."

"Something wrong?" he probed.

"It's, uh, just that . . ." The words stuck in my throat. I couldn't tell him I was struggling with my loyalty to someone else. A jerk named Jared.

"Tell you what," Sean began. "I'll make it easy, Holly. Think about it a couple of days, and if you don't show by, let's say, seven o'clock, I'll know you're not coming. How's that?" He looked positively adorable, almost boyish, as he cast his quizzical expression my way.

It wouldn't be easy deciding what to do between now and Christmas Eve, but I nodded in agreement.

"So you'll think about it?" He wasn't being pushy like Danny Myers had been, or flirtatious like Jared Wilkins. In many ways he reminded me of a surprising combination: Attentive yet hilarious Uncle Jack—and my handsome, sweet daddy. Adding to the fact that I was still totally

crushed over the master of two-time, Jared himself, the enticement of Sean twinkled on the
waves like a zillion stars.

"I'll think about it," I said, gazing up at Sean.
"I promise."

15

Right after supper I confronted Carrie in her room. "It wouldn't be so bad if this obsession you have with snooping was a one-time shot. I mean, if I had an older sister, who knows, maybe I'd snoop, too. But you . . . you never quit!" I sighed, anger building with each word.

Carrie looked repentant enough. Her lips were pursed together; her head hung low. "It's just so . . . so much fun," she responded, attempting to sound contrite. "I'm sorry, Holly. I'll never, ever do it again."

"I can't trust you," I said. "And how are you opening my diary without the key?"

She stared at me, her eyes wide. Pulling a toothpick out of her pocket, she held it up, her lower lip quivering like crazy. "This."

I snatched it out of her hand and raced to my room. Flinging the bedspread back, I uncovered my journal. With Carrie's toothpick, I picked the lock. "Amazing," I muttered, my anger subsiding only for an instant. Then I heard a sound and spun around.

Carrie had followed me and was crying. I faced the little snoop squarely. "If you ever so much as think twice about revealing any of the contents of this . . ." I waved the diary in her pixie face, breathing hard.

"Please, don't tell Mommy," she pleaded.

"I'll do whatever it takes to make you stop."

"Like what?" She was sobbing.

"Like getting you down on your knees to repent to God while I listen," I retorted.

"Just don't tell Mommy, okay?"

I studied her hard, and then the truth dawned. "Oh, I know what you're so worried about. It's Christmas, isn't it?"

Slowly, she nodded.

"You think you won't get any presents if Mom finds out."

She was silent, wiping her eyes. Carrie didn't believe in Santa Claus, but she was still worried. Who knows, something coal black could end up in her Christmas stocking next week when we celebrated in Dressel Hills.

"Silly girl." I shook my diary at her. "Do you promise to stay away from this?"

"I promise," she echoed.

Somewhat relieved, I waved her out of my room. Then I sprawled on the bed, reaching for a pen to record the events of the day. Having someone like Sean interested in me was so exciting. It helped ease the snooping incident with Carrie. Calmly, I relived the day of surfing again and again. Sean's every word, every gesture was embedded in my brain.

Comparing Sean with Jared was really dumb, but strange as it seemed, my thoughts turned back to Dressel Hills. Two-timing Jared to get even just wasn't my style. I mulled that idea for a while.

But he'd never find out, I argued with myself, imagining the fun of spending Christmas Eve on a beach bathed in moonlight. Perfect!

Upstairs I borrowed some gift wrap, a scissors, and tape from Saundra. Then heading down the hallway, I noticed Carrie whispering to Daddy in his study. There, among his classic books of poetry, he was quietly conversing with her.

Inching closer, I smelled the magic of old books mixed with Daddy's spicy cologne. The scent stopped me in my tracks. Then I heard his gentle laughter.

I slipped unnoticed into the room, investigating Carrie's face as an impish smile burst upon it. "What's going on?" I asked.

Daddy's face lit up like the white candles in

each of the windows. "Christmas secrets," he whispered.

"Never ask questions before Christmas," Carrie protested.

"Hmm," Daddy said. "Both my girls in the same room at the same time. Can it be?" He pulled me down on one of his knees while balancing giggly Carrie on the other. I placed the wrapping paper and scissors on his desk.

"It's gonna be such a cool Christmas," Carrie announced, eyeing the wrapping paper. "I can't wait!"

"Three more days?" Daddy teased. "We open gifts around here on Christmas Eve."

"Really? Christmas Eve?" I muttered, thinking of Sean's invitation.

"That's cool," shouted Carrie, racing off to tell Tyler, no doubt.

My tentative plans with Sean were at stake. "What time are we opening presents?" I asked, concerned.

Daddy patted my hand. "Don't you worry, honey; I'm sure we can work around your schedule."

Did he know about Sean's invitation? And if so, how? I turned to look for Carrie, the little rat. "Uh, excuse me a sec," I said, getting up.

"What's your hurry?" Dad asked.

"I need to talk to Carrie about something."

Daddy cleared his throat. I could tell by the look on his face he was about to defend her. "If you think Carrie let anything slip, you're wrong. Sean called while you and Saundra were cleaning up the kitchen."

This was news to me.

Daddy continued. "He asked permission to spend time with you."

"You're kidding." I was dumbfounded.

He leaned back in his chair as I stood up, facing him. I wondered what else he knew about my friendship with Sean. "A really terrific kid, that Sean Hamilton," he said, reaching for the newspaper. "It's good to develop friendships with lots of boys, Holly. You're awfully young to be tied down to one fellow."

I sighed. *How'd he know about Jared?*

"Mom says that, too," I said, picking up the bows and paper and stuff. "I, uh, have some presents to wrap now." I fled from the study, wondering if Carrie had blabbed the entire contents of my journal to Daddy.

Closing the door to my room, I switched on the clock radio beside the bed. Christmas songs, old and new, filled the room with cheer. As I wrapped my gifts, I allowed myself the luxury of Sean-thoughts.

I was nearly finished wrapping my purchases when I heard it. The strains of a familiar tune—

"Jingle Bell Rock." The jazzy song brought back memories of the Christmas party at Pastor Rob's house. Andie had played her rendition of it while Joy presented me with the secret-pal gift. Two hours later, I had witnessed Jared's gift-giving rendezvous behind the Christmas tree.

Flipping the knob on the radio, I refused to shed another tear over Jared Wilkins, King of Deceit!

Instead, I told my diary the latest delicious facts about Sean Hamilton, Prince a la Proper.

♥ ♥ ♥

The next day, Tyler delivered a stack of Christmas cards to the house. Three of them were addressed to me. One was from Mom and Uncle Jack, another from Andie, and the third was from none other than Jared.

I went to the kitchen, sliced the envelopes open with a letter opener, and raced downstairs to read in privacy. For some unknown reason, I pulled out Jared's card first. Enclosed was a letter.

Dear Holly-Heart,
*   Hope you're having fun with your California family. You'd better be, otherwise I'm missing you*

*for nothing. I wish we could've said good-bye
before you left. (Why'd you disappear like that?)*

*It won't be long and you'll be back in Colo-
rado. Thanks again for* A Heart Full of Poetry.
*It's outstanding and so are you! Please write soon.
Honestly, nothing's the same here with you gone.*
                                    Always,
                                    Jared

"What a con artist," I sneered, stuffing the
card and its contents into the envelope. I had
more important things to attend to than reading
lies from the pen of Jared Wilkins.

♥   ♥   ♥

At last, December twenty-fourth arrived.
Daddy and I spent the morning running errands
for Saundra. She'd ordered expensive trays and
platters and things. Never in a zillion years could
I imagine my mom spending so much money on
prepared food. But it was interesting and perfectly lavish, Daddy's new life.

"What do you think of California so far?"
Daddy shot the question to me as we waited in
bumper-to-bumper holiday madness.

"*This* stuff I can live without," I said, referring

to the traffic on all sides of us. "But the ocean's nice. So is the weather."

"And . . . what about the people?" he asked.

I wasn't sure what he was getting at. "The only people I really know here are you, Saundra, and Tyler."

"Tyler seems quite taken with you and Carrie." He took his foot off the brake, and the car inched forward a few feet.

"Tyler's a cool stepbrother," I said, wondering what he was going to ask next.

"And your stepmother?" He stared straight ahead.

"She's nice, actually. We, uh, had sort of a heart-to-heart talk the other day."

"I'm happy to hear that, Holly."

"There *is* something that bothers me about her, though."

He turned toward me, a question mark in his eyes.

"I understand she's not thrilled about praying." I felt hesitant about bringing this subject up. But it bugged me that Tyler thought Saundra would be upset if she caught him praying at mealtime.

Daddy took a deep breath. "Saundra was never one to entertain notions of a personal God," he said. "So she hasn't emphasized it with Tyler, either."

I jumped on that one. "But the God of the Bible *is* personal. I know Him, Daddy. And I know something else." I paused, thinking ahead. "God loved you and Saundra and Tyler, or He wouldn't have bothered sending Jesus to Earth as a baby. That's the bottom line—Christmas is about a personal God."

"I can see you believe this," he commented softly.

"With all of my heart," I answered.

"Well, I've been doing a lot of thinking about a book a friend gave me," he said with a twinkle in his eye. "It's by a fellow named St. Matthew."

I couldn't keep from grinning. "You're reading Matthew's gospel?"

He nodded.

"Daddy, that's fabulous," I said, giving his hand a little squeeze. "This has to be the best Christmas present ever!"

"Ah, but the day's not over," he hinted. I had no idea what was on his mind. But it *was* something. Something he seemed to have trouble keeping secret.

♥   ♥   ♥

After a sumptuous supper, Saundra insisted

on cleaning the kitchen herself. It was part of her Christmas gift to the family, she said. Dusk was falling fast, and Sean would be waiting.

I headed for the living room, where Carrie and Tyler were shaking presents. "You might break something," I scolded.

"Right," Carrie snapped. "You used to do it, too, before you got so mature."

Tyler grinned.

"It's almost dark," Carrie said without looking up. "What a great night for a walk on the beach."

Yep, she'd read that page in my diary all right.

"Sure is," I declared, leaving the holiday splendor of the living room for a peek through the telescope in Carrie's room. One quick look would tell me what I longed to know. I leaned over slightly, adjusting the focus.

Just as I thought. Sean Hamilton was definitely a reliable guy. Unlike someone else I knew.

I peered through the telescope a moment longer, bringing Sean closer . . . closer into view. I could almost reach out and touch his blue sweat shirt. The number thirty-four twinkled in the moonlight.

Then I raced to my room and closed the door. Rushing to the mirror, I checked my hair. Moving closer, I checked my makeup. Oh yeah, he wouldn't see much outside. Forget makeup.

Yikes—the moonlight! I ran into the bathroom and brushed some light-pink blush onto my already rosy cheeks.

Tucking my shirt into my jeans, I dashed around the room, pulling my tennies out of the closet. Was Sean still waiting? I reached down and tied my shoes. Then I leaped up and headed for the door.

Halfway up the stairs, I remembered I'd left my diary open on the bed for the world to see. Racing back to my room, I grabbed it, but my eyes caught a phrase I'd written weeks before. *Faithful, loyal, true*—the first stanza of one of the poems for Jared. Honest, heartfelt feelings in the form of poetry—what a terrific Christmas gift from a true friend. The true friend being me, of course.

And then it hit me. If I was so loyal and true, what was I doing meeting Sean? Just because Jared had broken his promise didn't mean I had to break mine. Did it?

I flicked off the lights and turned toward the windows overlooking the beach. A tall, dark form was tossing pebbles into the ocean. "I'm sorry, Sean," I whispered in the darkness. "Please understand." A warm feeling spread over me, and deep in my heart I knew I'd made the right choice.

Turning toward the door, I scurried up the

stairs. "Daddy," I called. "Let's open presents."

Carrie ran ahead of me. "Aren't you gonna meet Sean?" she asked.

"Not this time," I said. "Mind your own business."

"You'll never guess what Santa brought you," she said, giggling.

"Santa who?" I teased, following her.

"My lips are locked."

"That's a first," I muttered, heading down the hall to the festive living room.

16

I sat on the floor beside Tyler. A few presents were already piled up around him.

"Who would like to play Santa Claus?" Saundra asked, snuggling close to Daddy.

"I will," offered Carrie, hopping up. She scooted under the Christmas tree and began delivering the mountain of presents, one by one.

When all the gifts had been distributed, Daddy did an amazing thing. He reached for a Bible on the lamp table. Silently, he thumbed through it till he found Matthew 1:18. " 'This is how the birth of Jesus Christ came about,' " he began.

I noticed the startled look on Saundra's face. Tyler pulled restlessly at a red bow on one of his presents.

When Daddy came to the verse, "She will give birth to a son, and you are to give him the name Jesus, because he will save his people from their sins," I noticed Tyler look up. He was actually listening.

Shortly, Daddy was into chapter two, the part where the Magi came. It was almost like he couldn't find a stopping place. I glanced at Saundra. She sat silently as he spoke the wondrous words of Christmas.

In my heart, I sent a prayer heavenward.

Daddy continued, " 'On coming to the house, they saw the child with his mother Mary, and they bowed down and worshiped him. Then they opened their treasures and presented him with gifts of gold and of incense and of myrrh.' "

"Wow," Tyler chimed in. "So *that's* how it all got started."

Daddy finished reading, and then we began opening our presents, starting with the youngest. After Carrie, Tyler opened his gifts. He tore into my present to him—the book on creation. I held my breath.

"Hey . . . cool," Tyler exclaimed, paging through the book, then holding it high. "Thanks, Holly, now I can get some big questions answered."

Saundra didn't say a word.

It was my turn. I reached for a small, square box.

"Save that one for last," Carrie objected.

Daddy agreed. Something told me this was the secret he'd hinted about earlier.

I opened a present from Tyler and two with both Daddy's and Saundra's name on them. Finally I reached for the small gift. A mini card was attached. It read: "Happy Holly-days. Love, Daddy."

Gently, I pried the ends loose and pulled off the wrapping paper. Carefully, I lifted the lid.

Inside was my mother's gold locket!

Carrie covered her mouth. I stared at her, still amazed. Then she leaned against me, whispering in my ear. "Forgive me?"

Then I knew. "So that's why you were snooping around in my diary." Instantly, I comprehended what had transpired over the past week.

"So . . . what do you think?" Daddy asked, leaning forward.

"It's the best!" I cried, crawling over to thank him. When we hugged, I spotted the Bible on the lamp table, still open to Matthew. "Well, almost," I whispered.

"Here, why don't you wear it now, dear?" Saundra said, offering to help with the clasp.

I gathered up my hair and held it while she placed the long gold chain around my neck. "It's lovely," Saundra said, admiring it.

Br-r-ing! Tyler and Carrie raced to the phone. I stroked the heart locket, staring at the precious piece of jewelry. "Thank you, Daddy," I said. "I love it."

"And I love you," he said, eyes glistening.

Tyler ran into the living room. "It's long distance for you, Holly. Some boy named Jared."

Jared! I leaped up, heading for the privacy of the kitchen. *What's he calling about?* I wondered as I picked up the receiver. "Hello?"

"Merry Christmas, Holly-Heart." The sound of his voice made my broken heart sing.

"Thanks," I said softly, not sure how I should respond.

"Hey, what's wrong?" he prodded.

"What are you talking about?"

"Holly? Something's wrong—I can hear it in your voice."

"Everything's wrong," I blurted, peeking around the corner, checking for snoopers.

"Are you homesick? Is that it?"

"Not really," I said, hesitating. "I'm just so . . . well, surprised to hear your voice."

"It's Christmas Eve, isn't it?" he said dreamily. "I wish you were here. There's a candlelight service later. I'd rather be sitting with you at church than next to my parents."

"Or Paula, don't you mean?"

A long silence followed. I waited.

Slowly, Jared responded, "Did you say Paula?"

"She's nuts about you, but I'm sure you know

that by now." Deep inside, I was a wreck. His voice sounded so good to me, bringing with it all the old memories, the good times.

"I like *you*, Holly. Nothing's changed."

Taking a deep breath, I said, "But you gave her a Christmas present; isn't that a little misleading?"

"I didn't give Paula Miller a gift." He sounded dumbfounded.

"Yeah, I saw you at the party last week."

"You saw what?"

Then I explained, in great detail, the gift exchange I'd witnessed.

Laughter! Jared was laughing hysterically.

Finally I got his attention. "What's so funny?"

He tried to speak. "If that's all you're worried about, forget it. My secret pal, Shauna, was sick that night. I took her gift to the party for Paula to give to Shauna later."

I stood there speechless as his words sank in. What a fool I'd been. "You delivered Shauna's present to Paula? That's all it was?"

"Yep," Jared said.

"What about Paula's gift to you, the one at school?" By now, I sounded as jealous as a cat, but I was clawing for the truth.

"Somehow, Paula found out Billy Hill had gotten her name from you," he explained.

I smiled. "That's right, he and I traded names."

"Well, when Paula heard that Billy liked her, she decided to set up her own secret-pal exchange, using me as the delivery boy." Jared started to chuckle again. "In fact, at this moment, Billy still doesn't know who gave him that gift."

"Sneaky," I mumbled, feeling lousy for falsely accusing Jared in my heart, and in my diary. And Paula, too.

"Wait'll you see what I got you, Holly," Jared was saying.

"You bought me a present?"

"And you'll never guess what it is," he teased.

Daddy was motioning to me from the living room.

"I'd better not guess right now," I said, explaining that we were in the middle of our family gift-opening.

"Lucky you. I have to wait till morning," he said.

"I'll write, okay?"

"Can't wait," he said. "Bye, Holly."

"Thanks for calling, and Merry Christmas," I said before hanging up.

Still shocked at the truth of Jared's story, I made my way through the maze of crumpled

Christmas wrap as Saundra lit the gold candles on the mantel. What an amazing Christmas Eve this had turned out to be.

♥ ♥ ♥

With the problem of Jared cleared up, the second week at Daddy's house sped by faster than the first. He took us to Disneyland and Sea World, like he'd promised. It was so fabulous.

I didn't see Sean again. Tyler said he was probably busy with his older brother and his niece and nephew, who'd come home for Christmas. *Uncle* Sean. No wonder he was good with kids.

California had been lots of fun, but returning home to Dressel Hills was even better. On my first night back, I was helping Mom prepare supper when the doorbell rang.

A quartet of kids raced to investigate. Phil and Mark swung the door wide. Carrie and Stephie grabbed Jared's jacket—the visitor—fighting over who would get to hang it up.

Mom shooed everyone out of the living room, assigning table-setting chores to the door-greeters. Thank goodness for savvy moms.

"Welcome home, Holly-Heart," Jared said,

holding out a large silver box with a sprig of holly on top.

"Thanks," I said. "Should I open it?"

"Why not?"

Untying the bow, I looked up at him. Jared was grinning, his eyes twinkling mischievously.

When I opened the lid on the box, I gasped and turned red. It was a brown suede boot—just like the one I'd baptized in the toilet!

"It's the right boot," he whispered. "That's the one you needed."

I stared at him in disbelief. "Who told you?"

Just then, Stan emerged from the coat closet. "Sorry, little sister," John Wayne, alias Stan Patterson, remarked. "Couldn't help myself."

"Who else knows?" I demanded.

"The buck stops here, pilgrim," Stan crooned, pointing to the two of them—Jared and himself.

Then Jared reached into the boot and pulled out a teeny red box. "Voilà!"

"What's this?" I asked, delighted.

"Open it and see for yourself," Jared replied.

Happily, I opened the lid. Inside, a bottle of perfumed toilet water awaited. The word *Always*, in Jared's own handwriting, covered up the original brand name. I turned the dainty lid and put my nose down close, breathing in the fragrance. "Mmm, nice," I said, smiling at him.

With a single wink, Jared said it all.

Quickly dabbing perfume behind both ears, I began to hum "Jingle Bell Rock."

"Nice song," Jared said. He began to hum along, harmonizing with me.

I sighed happily. "Nice blend."

"No kidding," said Jared.

Even if I *had* been the slightest bit California crazy while I was gone for Christmas, I was definitely cured. Things were going to be fabulously fine now. I was perfectly sure.

♥ ♥ ♥

Don't miss HOLLY'S HEART #6,
Second-Best Friend
Available July 2002!

Holly's best friend, Andie, has a pen pal visiting from Austria—making Holly only second-best for a few weeks. Holly feels left out, and to make things worse, she has to give up Goofey, her beloved cat. No way will she let Pathetic Paula keep him. Will Holly overcome her jealousy before she ruins all of her relationships?

About the Author

Beverly Lewis loves writing stories with engaging characters and page-turning plots for her loyal readers. She remembers going on a trip with her family at Christmastime, leaving her girl friends (and one very cute boy friend behind). The holiday vacation was not nearly as agonizing for Beverly as it was for Holly Meredith in this book, but she *does* remember eagerly looking forward to returning home.

Going home is still the best part of any trip for Beverly, no matter where she and her family travel. "I always enjoy getting away for a while when I'm not writing," she says. "But toward the end of each vacation, I start counting the hours to our return . . . and to starting my next book!"

Also by Beverly Lewis

PICTURE BOOKS

Cows in the House   Annika's Secret Wish
Just Like Mama

THE CUL-DE-SAC KIDS
Children's Fiction

The Double Dabble Surprise   Tarantula Toes
The Chicken Pox Panic   Green Gravy
The Crazy Christmas Angel Mystery   Backyard Bandit Mystery
No Grown-ups Allowed   Tree House Trouble
Frog Power   The Creepy Sleep-Over
The Mystery of Case D. Luc   The Great TV Turn-Off
The Stinky Sneakers Mystery   Piggy Party
Pickle Pizza   The Granny Game
Mailbox Mania   Mystery Mutt
The Mudhole Mystery   Big Bad Beans
Fiddlesticks   The Upside-Down Day
The Crabby Cat Caper   The Midnight Mystery

ABRAM'S DAUGHTERS
Adult Fiction

The Covenant

THE HERITAGE OF LANCASTER COUNTY
Adult Fiction

The Shunning   The Confession
The Reckoning

OTHER ADULT FICTION

The Postcard
The Crossroad

October Song

The Redemption of Sarah Cain

Sanctuary*

The Sunroom

www.BeverlyLewis.com

*with David Lewis

REAL LIFE,
REAL FAITH!

Stuck in the Sky
Opportunity Knocks Twice
Good-Bye to All That

Fast Forward to Normal
Double Exposure
Grasping at Moonbeams

Do you have what it takes to be a Brio Girl?

Come join the fun with Jacie, Hannah, Solana, Becca, Tyler, and the rest of their friends as these teens live life with faith…and fun. The issues they face—keeping friendships and family important, improving their witness, dedicating themselves to purity—are the same as in your own life. Have fun right along with the Brio girls as they struggle through challenges and build life-long friendships.